Bound By Vines

Bound By Vines

G. R. McWhorter

Bound By Vines

© G.R. McWhorter, 2022

Published by Artifix Press, 2023

ISBN: 9798398746334

All rights reserved. No part of this book may be reproduced in any form or by any electronic or mechanical means, including information storage and retrieval systems, without written permission from the publisher or author, except in the case of a reviewer, who may quote brief passages embodied in critical articles or in a review.

This book is a work of fiction. Any references to historical events, real people, or real locales are used fictitiously. Any resemblance to actual events, or persons, living or dead, is coincidental.

Bound By Vines

Chapter One

"Where there is no wine, there is no love." - Euripides

The hot sun of June in Southern California was beating down on the roof of the small, vintage, Volkswagen car driven by Lea Baudin as she left San Diego and headed north into the Temecula Valley. As she drove, the sea breezes dissipated and gave way to the warmer inland air and the scent of orange blossoms and spring flowers. Lea had finally stopped crying, but her eyes were still red and puffy from her dried tears as she got off the freeway and headed toward the winery region of Temecula. She passed many large, multi-million dollar, wineries, but hardly noticed them as she made her way deeper into the back of the region. Lea finally turned down a difficult-to-spot side road, leaving the asphalt of the main road for this dirt road. She knew this road well. She knew every bump, twist, and turn.

After a one-mile dusty drive, she arrived at the long driveway and drove up to the main house. She was finally home. It all looked the same to her as it did when she last visited about four months ago. 'Why didn't I visit sooner,' she thought to herself. The

Mediterranean-style ranch home with its whitewashed walls and red tiled roof. The large bougainvillea plants around the walls with their hot pink flowers in full bloom. The grape vines are in neat rows on the sides and rear of the home with their delicate fruit just starting to fatten up in the summer heat. She once felt the sun was kissing every grape and filling them with energy and sweetness. It was all her reality growing up, but now it seemed like a dream turned nightmare. As she parked her car by the front door, she steadied herself. She knew she had challenging work ahead and her crying time was over. She would have to carry on the best she could.

Her cellphone rang. It was her dorm-mate Roxy.

"Hey Roxy. What's up?"

"I just wanted to check on you. You were pretty broken up when you left and I was worried if you were okay to drive."

"I'm fine. I actually just made it here."

"Okay. Good. Is there anything I can do for you?"

"No. I probably won't be back for a few days if you want to let others know. I'll be fine. I just…" she fought back the sobbing, "…need to deal with all this."

"I know." They said their goodbyes and hung up.

With resolve, Lea finally got out of the car and walked up to the door. There was only a slight hesitation before she opened the door and walked in. She stood in the foyer and looked around at her parents' home, where she had grown up. She took a deep breath and started to go from room to room, cautiously, as if in a daze. The house seemed so empty and lifeless to her. The warmth and joy seemed absent now. No one appeared to be home. She walked out onto the back porch and spotted Manuel far out along one of the grape rows. Lea spotted Isobel, Manuel's wife, a little way off to one side of the house doing some work in her small vegetable garden. Still, in a daze, Lea started walking toward Isobel. As she got nearer to the vegetable garden, Isobel saw Lea and dropped her trowel, and ran toward her with outstretched arms.

"Aye, mi hija...mi pobre hija..."

Isobel enveloped Lea in her warm arms and both of them dropped to the ground and cried on each other's shoulders. Manuel came running up, but stood a few feet away, not sure what to do, but he finally knelt and placed a reassuring hand on Lea's other shoulder. The three sobbed as the afternoon sun wore on and the only other sound was from a light breeze blowing through the vineyard. Lea told the couple she was not ready to talk about the sudden, and unexpected, death of her parents just yet. She needed time to acclimate to it and the couple understood.

After a while, Isobel and Manuel took Lea back inside the house and up to her room for a nap. As Lea slept, Manuel brought her luggage inside and Isobel proceeded to cook dinner. When Manuel returned, Isobel told him, "She will need some good comfort food tonight and lots of love."

"Yes, we will fill her with warm food and our love."

They both knew tonight would be hard for Lea as it was her first-time home since the death of her parents.

Isobel and Manuel Ontiveros had first come to Chateau Baudin Winery in the late 1980s as grape pickers. They had illegally crossed the border from Mexico into California and lived poorly until finding work at the Baudin family winery. Alain Baudin was a kindly man who had taken to the young Mexican couple as they, like him, believed in the American Dream and sought a better life and were not afraid to work hard for it. Alain saw a bit of himself in the couple as he watched how they struggled yet maintained a strong work ethic. Alain regularly offered them better pay and benefits as they continued working for the winery. Isobel and Manuel were fiercely loyal to Alain and his wife Claire as they felt valued and treated well by the Baudin family. They were both witness to Claire's pregnancies and the births of both Rose and Lea. Isobel and Manuel helped take care of the girls as they grew up and played in the vineyards their grandfather Alphonse had established.

Grandfather Alphonse was a French Jew whose family had a small vineyard in France and lost it when the Nazis overran France during World War II. Alphonse was one of the few lucky Jews. His family understood what was happening to Jews and they had their whole family baptized Catholic as the Nazis gained power. So, Alphonse, who had been baptized Catholic, was able to hide among other Catholic children at a distant boarding school. The rest of his family were not as lucky and were taken away to concentration camps never to be seen again. Alphonse was a survivor and after years of hiding, he grew into a hardworking young man who could not wait to escape to the United States after the Nazis were beaten and he could safely leave France. He had saved his money and was able to immigrate and settle in Southern California.

He chose California because of all the Hollywood films he had seen as a child, which filled him with hope and helped him get through tough times. Alphonse figured if a poor British child with a name like Archibald Leach could move to California and transform himself into the mega-millionaire world-renowned movie star Cary Grant, then he too could do well there. Several years of hard work, determination, and adding to his initial savings followed. Knowing vineyards and farm work, Alphonse had no problem finding jobs within California's agricultural industry. He took whatever jobs paid the best, sometimes working with oranges or his final job as a foreman on an avocado farm in Fallbrook. No matter what he did, he always held a desire to get back to working with grapes.

While making deliveries of Avocados to San Diego, he met another French expatriate named Antoinette. She was also of Jewish descent and her family had fled France just before the Nazis invaded. Her family was affluent, but her parents had been elderly and her father passed away shortly after arriving in the United States. She still had her elderly mother, who she took care of. As things happen, Alphonse was taken by this stunning French girl who not only understood him, but also had been through some similar challenges. Before long, he asked for her hand in marriage and soon they had one son, Alain.

The little family, which included Antoinette's mother, lived frugally, and saved as much money as they could. Within a few years, Alphonse was able to buy some acreage in the Temecula Valley in what would eventually become wine country. He knew where grapevines would do well and he bet on this area. Others did too, and although it got harder and harder to buy adjacent acreage, he established a sizable vineyard through his hard work.

Temecula Valley was a great place for growing wine grapes. The region had a closer solar intensity, due to it being at higher angle toward the sun than places like Napa, and a lower rainfall too. With less rain, there was less of a chance of rain interrupting the harvest and morning mists tended to last until late morning which helped with ground moisture. This coastal mountain range made for sunny days and cool nights, which are good for grape growing along with soil composed of decaying granite.

    The Baudin vineyard was a private concern as it developed with wine being made just for family and friends. Alphonse had kept his other job while working on his own land during his off-hours. His son grew strong and helped with the work including building and expanding the family home on the land. Unfortunately, Antoinette's mother did not live to see its completion as she passed away. Like any other family, the Baudin's had their 'ups and downs,' but no matter what, they pushed on.

    His son, Alain, eventually grew up and married a French girl named Claire, who he had met while on a vacation-visit in France. As the years passed, Alphonse and Antoinette passed away from old age and Alain and Claire inherited the small private winery. During this time, the couple was blessed with children of their own, Rose and Lea. When the girls were toddlers, the Temecula Valley started experiencing a renaissance of sorts with local wineries cropping up and this newfound interest in California wine. Alain saw how other vineyards, like the Callaway Vineyard and Winery, were starting to bottle and sell wine. He decided it was time the family vineyard went commercial. A lot more hard work, as well as trial and error occurred, but the winery started selling bottles of wine. They were struggling, but they were able to make enough money that at least they were their own bosses and could afford to keep the roof over their heads.

Both Lea, and her older sister Rose, enjoyed a happy childhood running up and down among the vines and playing hide-and-seek in the family barn and so on. They had all the grapes they could eat and they both enjoyed the outdoors and basking in the warm California sun. As they grew into teens, they viewed the winery as their parents' business and wanted to see what the world had to offer them. Both girls spent as much time as they could away from the winery and eventually moved out altogether. It wasn't that they disliked the winery, they just wanted to find interests that were their own. They loved that their parents had a small, but beautiful winery, but they always thought of it as their parents' thing. Like a hobby they made money out of.

Lea and her sister Rose had a lot of fun together and made many great childhood memories, but as they got older, they drifted apart. Rose was older so her tastes matured while Lea seemed like an entitled brat to her. They began to fight more and more as Rose felt Lea was always trying to sabotage everything from her personal things to events they had to attend together. The fun times of the past had given way to petty squabbles. One day, Lea might use up all of Rose's make-up playing 'model' without asking. The next day, Rose might tell on Lea for kissing a boy behind the barn or trying cigarettes, and so on. The sisters became bitter adversaries and each could not wait until they could get away from the other, much to their parents' dismay.

    Rose had left the home first, as she pursued her studies, but soon thereafter Lea found an apartment she could share with friends in San Diego and spent as much time as she could at the beach or in nightclubs dancing. She learned how to surf and was good enough at it she started giving lessons for some quick money. Eventually, she tried to start a surfboard lesson and rental business, but when this failed, her parents bailed her out on the condition she went back to school to get a degree. Several of her friends went to San Diego State University so she went there too to be with them. Lea started studying history and art in an undergraduate program at San Diego State University, where she also moved into the dorms with her friend Roxy Carpani.

    Lea's older sister, Rose, had received her Juris Doctorate and was practicing law as a junior lawyer at a high-powered firm in New York. Neither of the girls had ever thought of running the winery and believed their parents would eventually retire from the wine business and sell it off. After all, the winery had never been able to compete with the much larger ones nearby. The Chateau Baudin Winery was considered a boutique winery at best. Only a few thousand bottles were produced annually for sale at local independent stores, and farmer's markets, and a few shipped to daring wine aficionados who were always looking for a new wine. The girls never thought of the winery as much more than their parents' business-slash-hobby.

    Running the winery came to a sudden end for Alain and Claire one night as they were on their way home from a restaurant. Alain believed in taking Claire out on a 'date night' at least once every other week. He believed courtship did not end with marriage and wooing his wife was part of loving her. They had a wonderful steak dinner in Old Town Temecula and were heading home when a drunk driver crossed into their lane and hit them head-on, killing the couple instantly. Somehow the drunk driver managed to get his car started and disappeared into the night. There was one elderly man who saw what happened to tell the story to the police, but he didn't see much or get any helpful details other than the driver had a black truck with a sticker that said 'Git-R-Done,' which was a popular redneck saying.

    Both sisters had been called the next morning by the sheriff's department and told what had happened. Lea and Rose both acted similarly as they went into shock and said little. They were alike in how they both needed time to process tough information like this. Because of their mental and physical distance, they did not think to call each other. They both knew it was time to get home as soon as possible and they would meet up there. They were not in a mind for rational thought as they made plans in an almost auto-pilot sort of daze.

    Lea had not been home in almost four months as she enjoyed her life in San Diego. At twenty-five, she felt she was finally finding herself. She was a vivacious and exceedingly attractive young woman. At five-foot-five, she often felt she was the perfect height for all the things she tried as she could easily fit in wetsuits, sports cars, or whatever. Her bright blue eyes and honey-colored hair were nice features, but her smile and her dimples were truly dazzling to people who met her.

    Isobel looked in on Lea as she slept and thought to herself 'What a beautiful young woman she had become from the little child in pigtails who always seemed covered in dirt.' She was going to wake Lea for dinner, but decided to let her sleep instead. She knew it must be tough losing both parents at once and felt bad for both Baudin girls. She wondered how Rose was taking the news. The police had told her and Manuel that they had contacted the girls so she knew they were on their way. She also wondered why Rose was not yet here and hoped for her arrival soon. Rose could help her sister Lea in grieving. Isobel also knew there were many tough decisions to be made about the winery and both girls would need to rely on one another and share their strengths. She closed the door to Lea's bedroom and gave a silent prayer in the hallway for Rose to arrive soon.

Chapter Two

"Give me wine to wash me clean of the weather-stains of cares." - Ralph Waldo Emerson

It was a tense moment in the courtroom. The judge glanced over to the prosecuting attorney and asked; "Is there anything else you wish to add to this case?"

"No, your Honor. The prosecution rests." came the quick reply from the female attorney. The judge looked over and shuffled some papers on his desk, cleared his throat, then addressed the jury.

"Members of the jury, you have heard witness statements relevant to this case and have had copies of all pertinent documents to look over. The court asks you, at this time, to retreat to jury chambers and deliberate the case. Please take as long as you need. Once you have made a majority decision, please notify the bailiff, and wait for the court to ask for your return. Thank you for your service once again. Please follow the bailiff at this time."

The female attorney sat confidently knowing she had done a great job in explaining the evidence and prosecuting the case against such a large company as BioBlast, a social media giant that had been selling off the personal information of its users. When the verdict came back and was read by the Jury Foreman as "Guilty" she was not surprised. She stood up with her briefcase and left the courtroom. Although she was five-foot-seven without her heels, she felt as if she were seven-foot-tall as she walked out of the courthouse and was besieged by reporters. She was always a favorite with reporters as she was still a very young-looking twenty-nine years old and had long, silky brunette hair and big blue eyes like her sister. She also had those same dazzling dimples as her sister, but that is where the similarities ended. She was not as 'happy-go-lucky' as her younger sister. She viewed her little sister as a latter-day hippie. A true free-spirit who had no idea of what it was like to carve out a place in the 'real world.'

    Rose Baudin kept strict discipline with herself. She believed in regular exercise, healthy eating, getting chores done, and always being punctual to every appointment no matter how trivial. Her idea of punctuality was to be at least ten minutes early everywhere she needed to be. This often upset her boyfriends as they would find themselves with her waiting for stores to open or arriving at places before everyone else they had to meet. It was this self-discipline which made it tough for her to have long-lasting relationships. Most men found her too demanding, but in her defense, she tended to find most men too lazy and apathetic about self-discipline and punctuality.

After answering all of the reporter's questions and smiling for a few photos on the courthouse steps, she grabbed a taxi and headed to her loft apartment. While people living outside of a major city like New York might view her loft as rather small, it was spacious enough for her. It had a large common area with a small kitchen in one corner and two bedrooms. One bedroom was where she slept and the other bedroom was mainly used for storage of bulky stuff like file boxes from past legal cases, scuba diving gear, and bicycle equipment. It was in the large common room where she spent most of her time. She had made herself a workout area in one corner with a treadmill and a small weight set and a few other pieces of exercise equipment. In another corner, she had some file cabinets and her desk, where she usually worked on her laptop. She had a sectional couch and coffee table in the middle of the space. These sat on top of a large area rug. She had a large screen television in the middle of the wall facing across from the couch. Like most loft apartments, she had a small balcony where she kept two chairs for sitting when the weather was good and a small barbecue tucked in the back of one corner. The barbecue was used about once a year, usually around the 4th of July, and was mainly a home for spiders the rest of the year.

    After changing, Rose went into the kitchen and poured herself a glass of Chateau Baudin chardonnay, which she took over to her couch. As she sipped the buttery-tasting wine, she thought of how a nice glass of wine always helped to soothe her nerves or give her strength whenever she was feeling blue.

Automatically, she grabbed the remote and clicked on some light classical music. She sat and stared at a picture on the wall of her mother and father and allowed herself to cry for the first time since receiving the call about the death of her parents early in the morning, just before court. Because of her court case, she had to suppress her feelings all day and only now did she give in to them.

"Mom...Dad..." was all she could mutter as she sobbed uncontrollably, her wine spilling on the couch. She cried alone for hours and managed to drink some of the wine as she reminisced about good times with her family and wondered what she would have to do next. She knew there would be many calls to make and she would have to ask her law firm to take some time off. She had taken a few days off last December to see her parents and she suddenly realized that was the last she had seen or talked to them and the tears started all over again.

Until she fell asleep, she only thought of her parents and herself. She never thought about what her sister might be going through. Rose and Lea had been distant for the last seven years after Rose moved to New York. They rarely exchanged phone calls or emails except during holidays and even those communications were never comfortable like the call she made for Lea's birthday.

"Hey Squirt, happy birthday!"

"Thanks."

"You must have some fun plans for today I bet?"

"Not really. My friends want to hang out at the beach today and have a bonfire and drum-circle when it gets dark. Should be fun I guess."

"Well, don't get too wasted. You don't want to get caught driving when you're drunk or stoned."

"Go to Hell, Rose!" Lea hung up.

After the call, Rose realized what she said to her sister might've been perceived badly, but there was truth she was trying to share and save her sister from trouble. This was often the problem. Rose tried to tell Lea how to live, believing she was helping, and Lea felt she knew enough and didn't need to her sister's criticism wrapped up as advice.

It would not be until the morning before she finally remembered Lea and wondered what she was doing and feeling right now. She tried to keep her thoughts about Lea positive, but they tended to slide to the negative. Rose wondered if Lea even knew about their parents yet. She had images of Lea, her beach bum sister, in Hawaii, or some exotic place, drinking Mai Tais and chasing, or being chased, by half-naked men. Lea might still be oblivious to everything going on. Rose felt she would need to fly out to California right away, assess the situation, and try to reel in her bohemian sister for some help in dealing with her parents' estate.

    Rose spent the next day making plans. She was a woman of action. She did not like procrastination with herself or with others. She called the firm and they immediately offered her two weeks of bereavement time off. She had just won a big case and had not yet been assigned another one so the firm was fine with her taking the time off. She booked an early flight for California, leaving the next morning. She packed, paid a few pressing bills, and proceeded to close up her loft. She was grieving so much that everything she did was dreamlike to her. It was like she was inside of a bubble somehow walking along the bottom of the ocean. Things whizzed around her, but she was in her bubble and everything outside the bubble lacked focus for her. Everything was abstract in some way and she felt she would never be able to fall asleep, but miraculously she finally dozed off out of exhaustion. She had cried and been depressed all day. Her body forced her to recharge.

    Rose marveled at herself, realizing she was finally on a plane heading to California. Her efficient and responsible side kicked in as if on autopilot. She had everything arranged. Before the flight, she remembered to rent a car for when she arrived at Ontario Airport. She would pick up the rental car and drive straight to her family's winery in Temecula. She used the maps app on her phone and saw the drive would take exactly one hour. She was a practical woman and planned ahead. On the flight, all her energy went to planning how to rope in her wild sister and the future of the Chateau Baudin Winery.

Meanwhile, in Temecula, Lea, Isobel, and Manuel were trying to enjoy the beautiful weather and being back in each other's company. "What a spectacular day!" observed Manuel out loud. He was speaking to himself as much as to the ladies. Isobel's only reply was "We must thank the Lord for each day." Lea just sat on the back patio looking over the neat rows of vines which glistened brightly in the early morning sun. She thought to herself how good it felt to smile again as she sipped her coffee. Isobel and Manuel were the closest people she had to family now. Lea knew they would never be surrogate parents, but they would be trusted friends and loved ones forever. The group sat drinking their coffee as they enjoyed the early morning warm rays of the sun and listened to the sing-song chirping of birds.

Being on the back patio, they did not hear the car pull up into the driveway. Rose sat in the rental car and took a moment to stare at her parents' home. She had grown up here and it felt strange to her to see the place knowing that her parents would not be inside. Tears started welling up in her eyes, but she quickly dabbed them with a tissue and forced herself into control. She knew she had to be tough and strong during this time for everyone's sake. She stepped out of the car and decided to head straight inside without taking her luggage out. When her hand touched the door handle, she froze. She wasn't going to cry, but she just could not bring herself to go inside yet. She decided to walk around the house and look over the vineyard. She knew her parents had worked hard to cultivate the land and had been so proud of their vines as they grew and yielded grapes. She had played among the vines as a young girl and had grown to understand her parents' love for their little winery. She turned toward the patio and saw the group sitting there.

"Hey, guys…" was all she could mumble.

"Oh…Hey! Rose!" was all that Lea could get out as she leaped to embrace her sister in a long hug. Isobel joined in too with Manuel only able to put a consoling hand on Rose's shoulder. Rose had promised herself she would not cry anymore, but as the tears flowed from everyone else, Rose's eyes started to water and she joined the group in a good cry.

Chapter Three

"Wine is constant proof that God loves us and loves to see us happy." - Benjamin Franklin

Isobel had made a huge dinner with enough machaca, rice, and beans for everyone along with a side of prickly pear cactus pads called nopales. Both Rose and Lea had grown up with Isobel's cooking and traditional Mexican food was more their comfort food than the light French dishes their mother and father knew how to cook. After dinner, everyone went to bed early. It had been a long day of catching up with stories of each other's lives and sharing remembrances of the recently deceased Alain and Claire. In their bed, Isobel and Manuel held each other and chatted about the girls being home again.

"Manuel, I don't know what to feel. I am so happy the girls are home, but then I am so sad about the reason why they had to come home."

"Querida, I know. It is a tough time for us all. All we can do is be supportive and share our love with them. They will be the ones who will need to work things out and make tough decisions."

"Do you think the will keep the winery?"

"Quién sabe...who knows. I hate to even think about it. I hope they will keep it and run it together, but they are very different. If I had to guess, I would think Lea would be the one to sell for many reasons.

She is young and sometimes foolish being the main reason."

"Yes…" Isobel was getting drowsy in Manuel's arms. "We will see what the future brings."

"Yes, my love." He kissed her forehead as his wife drifted off to sleep.

Everyone in the home went through their motions in an almost zombie-like state as a few days passed before the funeral of Alain and Claire. The sisters hardly talked to each other and when they did, they were often curt with one another. They did manage to stay civil with each other as they readied their emotions for the funeral. It was a sunny Sunday when their parents were laid to rest. Isobel and Manuel had taken care of hosting a post-funeral reception for mourners. Everything went off without a hitch, and Rose and Lea were quickly left alone to get over their grief. After a couple of days, both young women started to emerge from their rooms and began returning to normalcy, although tinged with sadness. Rose's two weeks of bereavement were almost over and she would soon have to return to New York and resume her law career and pursue new cases or else ask for a little more time away. To Rose, there seemed so much to consider. She fell asleep indecisive about what to do next.

Today was a new day as Rose got up to greet the dawn. After a quick shower and putting on some jeans and a T-shirt, she went downstairs to see who was up. Isobel was cooking breakfast and singing along to a song by Beatriz Adriana, a famous Mexican singer in the ranchera style. *'Te sientes muy guapo...Te sientes galán...Pero lo que eres es un pobre holgazán...'* Rose decided not to disturb her and went out to the vineyard where she found Manuel removing leaves from vines. He was originally the foreman, but now that her father was gone, he would have to act as head vintner too.

    She knew from years of helping her father, before she became an attorney, that removing leaves helped the ripening process as the sun could reach the grapes and reduced the chance for disease developing under the leaves, and also allowed for faster drying after a morning dew. All of this was important in growing the largest, sweetest, and healthiest grapes to be made into one of the Baudin select wines. As she watched Manuel from the top terrace, she realized that the man who she once played with and worked alongside, as a child amongst the vines, was getting older. His hair was gray and he was not as fast as he used to be. She wondered if Manuel and his wife had any plans for retirement or if her father had set anything up for them. There were so many details she would need to discover, and soon now that her parents were gone.

    "Good morning, Manuel!"

"Ah...Good morning to you Rose!" He waved and smiled before returning to the vines. She walked out to join him.

"Manuel, I know there is so much I need to figure out, but tell me...How are the grapes this year?" She had spent long hours conversing with this man as a child and even into her teens. She was able to open-up to him and deeply appreciated his simple wisdom and insight. Without stopping from his work, he was always able to hold long conversations with her.

"Rose, the grapes are fine. They are as good as last year. Do not worry about the grapes as long as I am here to tend them. As far as things you 'need to figure out,' remember you are not alone mi hija. You have a sister who can help carry your burdens. You two will make things work."

"I don't think I can count on Lea. She is just a kid...my little sister. She isn't even finished with school...getting her degree. Everything for her has just been all fun and games up to now. Beach parties, beer bashes..."

Manuel hesitated from his work and cut her short. "Listen, she is your mother and father's child too. She is smart and has many talents, just like you. You two will need each other now, more than ever. Combine your strengths. You must believe in each other."

Rose silently contemplated this for a moment until Isobel called to them to come inside for breakfast.

Her thoughts of Lea faded as she and Manuel went inside the large ranch house and joined Isobel and Lea at the breakfast table. Isobel made huevos rancheros with fresh orange juice from the one orange tree at the front of the house. Other than the tinkling of plates and other breakfast table sounds, the group talked very little. It wasn't until Isobel started clearing the now empty plates when Lea spoke up.

"Rose, I know we have a lot to discuss now that our mom and dad are gone. Have you given any thought about selling the vineyard?"

Rose quickly looked up from her plate and met her sister's eyes with a burning glare of anger.

"What the hell Lea? Mom and dad are barely gone and you're already thinking we should sell everything! Our whole lives have been tied to this vineyard. This was their dream!"

"Yes, but is it ours? I mean, is the vineyard *our dream*? You're a big-shot lawyer in New York now. You rarely came back to visit over the last few years. You have a whole other life now and I don't think I can run this place on my own. No offense Manuel and Isobel. You two are amazing, but there is so much to take care of. Are we really up to that?" Lea had glanced at the older couple before turning back to her sister who was looking absently at the checkered pattern of the tablecloth as if frozen in thought.

Manuel and Isobel had looks of shock slowly turning into indignation, yet remained quiet. They knew what the sisters were like and knew it was best to let them argue and reach what is the right decision on their own unless their opinions are asked for. In some rare instances, they would interject their own wisdom, but only after the girls had exhausted themselves in arguing and needed a way to move forward.

Although Manuel and Isobel were feeling worried and annoyed by this talk, they also knew the final decision of what would ultimately become of the vineyard would be up to the girls. They would need to be patient and pray the right answer would present itself. Manuel ambled back out to take care of the vines and Isobel left the dishes to soak and disappeared into the house.

Rose was seething. She remained quiet for a full two minutes in sheer anger and afraid of what she might say to Lea. She could not help herself and let loose her fury in words.

"Lea, you are such a flake! You have always been a sponge to mom and dad. You never even tried to understand business or anything! You were always asking them for money to fund your stupid ideas, never paying back a dime or realizing how much you were throwing away! I remember when mom and dad helped you set up a surfing school. You thought you'd get rich quickly by offering surfing lessons. So, they funded a beach shack and supplied you with wetsuits, surfboards, and who knows what else. The big joke was that you are not even a good surfer! Your students took advantage of you by not paying and your equipment started disappearing. They had to bail you out of that failed venture. And your schooling? What a fucking joke! Most people finish a bachelor's degree in four years, but it's been almost six years now and you're not even close. You have no concept of deadlines or getting work done. I should sell the vineyard because it would be too much for us together, but you don't deserve the money you would get out of it. You would just lose it like you do all the time with everything else you try to do."

Lea's eyes were welling up and tears started streaming down her face. When she was little, she might run away from her older sister after a chiding like this, but this time she knew she had to stand up to her. There was just no other way. Her delicate chin twitched as she fought back the sobbing and tried to reply through her tears.

"Rose!...Yes...I've never been the perfect daughter like you. You were always so efficient and studious that you got through college and law school quickly. You always worked and supported yourself, but you also had no friends and you rarely checked in on mom and dad once you moved to New York and became a hot-shot lawyer! You might be smarter than me and better at making a career than me, but no one likes you! You are too stiff and rigid! You will probably be a spinster because you'll never find a guy who will live up to your exacting standards! I might have had financial help from mom and dad, but I always visited them and shared my love and time with them. What did you ever do for them? You were never around as an adult and you know so little about them and their dreams."

Rose, who had met Lea's gaze during this diatribe, tore her eyes away. She could not look at Lea. She knew her sister was right and Lea's words stung her heart. The two sisters sat, fighting back tears as the silence became pregnant with unspoken emotions. Both of the girls were stubborn and it was usual for Lea to give in as she knew her sister was even more stubborn than her. Lea stood up and walked over to her sister. Rose, still seated with arms crossed, looked up at her with burning hatred in her eyes. Lea slumped down in front of her sister and embraced her from a kneeling position, sinking her head into her sister's lap. Rose looked down at her, unmoved, thinking to herself 'Here she goes. Typical dramatic flake behavior.' After a minute, Lea looked up at Rose with a sincerity in her eyes that almost disarmed Rose. Rose turned her head to stare at the wall as Lea spoke.

"Rose, I know we are two very different people and I'm scared. What do we know about grapes…vineyards…bottling…selling…wine. What do we know? Yes, it would be easy to sell. I'm smart enough to know that and I know that none of what mom and dad built here was what we have built for ourselves. I'm a student who is still trying to find my place in society...in life. You are a celebrated lawyer. It makes sense to me that we should sell. If we don't sell, can we really keep this going? Do we really want to keep this going?"

Slowly, Rose looked at her sister and in uncharacteristic fashion, broke down crying.

"I...don't...*sob*...know...*sob*, but I loved mom and dad! I feel terrible I have been so distant. I had to make my own way! I needed to pursue my dream! Now I miss them and can only think that somehow, we need to keep their dream alive. I don't...*sob*...know what to do!"

Lea had rarely seen her sister cry and this caused her to start crying too. Before long, even Isobel and Manuel were tearing up. Lea remained kneeling by her sister until Rose finally uncrossed her arms and hugged her sister back tightly.

They all sat in the kitchen for quite a while before Rose mumbled something about how they both needed to think things over and excused herself. Lea watched her go. Rose went to her room and flopped onto her bed and cried herself to sleep. Lea left the house and took a hike on some adjacent property that had not yet been developed. The girls would make a decision soon. They both knew they had to, but what would be the best solution? They were not farmers...not vintners. It was a tough decision and both girls were filled with frustration and trepidation about what any decision might hold for them both.

The day turned to night. The girls avoided each other, but they both knew Isobel would eventually call them together for dinner. At exactly five in the evening, Isobel sought out each girl and her husband and told them dinner was ready. Rose started to protest that she was not hungry. Isobel was used to her stubbornness and had made chili verde burritos with fresh guacamole and chips for dinner knowing this was her favorite dish. A dish Rose would not be able to refuse. Manuel was already seated when Lea came and sat down at the dinner table. Rose and Isobel arrived shortly and sat. All were silent as Isobel led them in a quick prayer as was normal at dinnertime. All said "amen" and then the food and a nice tempranillo red wine started passing around. Manuel and Isobel made small talk during the meal and the girls rarely interjected other than a small noise expression or word of affirmation. Isobel had outdone herself with the chili verde. She had even made fresh flan for dessert. Before the girls had finished their flan, Isobel looked at both of them and spoke up.

"Girls. Rose…Lea…Your parents were the nicest people Manuel and I have ever known. They helped us to gain citizenship and they gave us a home when others were not quick to. They may not have always been perfect, but in one way they were. They loved you both very dearly. Manuel and I have watched both of you grow from newborn babies into the young women you are now. We also love you very much. You two must make a decision, but know that whatever you decide also affects Manuel and me. That is all I have to say except that Manuel and I are eager to know what you wish to do so we can plan. And don't worry about us. No matter what you decide, we will be okay."

Isobel finished and smiled at both girls. Rose and Lea looked as if they wanted to start crying again as they locked eyes with the smiling Isobel. Manuel stayed quiet toying with his flan. He was afraid of what the girls might say. He knew Isobel was braver at discussions like this than him and he was glad she was opening up the talk. Slowly, Rose and Lea looked at each other. They met each other's gaze. Lea spoke up first.

"I'm game if you are. We can always try."

"Ye...Yes. We can try, but only if you two stay on to help and show us how." Rose looked quickly from her sister to the couple.

Isobel, still smiling, said; "Of course, we will, silly! Did I not just say that Manuel and I love you both? We would not dream of leaving you two to run the winery without our help too!"

After that, it was hard to know who got up first and started hugging whom. The decision had been made. The Chateau Baudin Winery was created out of love by Alphonse and Claire Baudin and it would remain for now through the love of their two children and a couple who had befriended their parents. These four were united by Alphonse's dream of making good wine, but they were also united by love and the happiness of being a family...together.

Chapter Four

"Sorrow can be alleviated by good sleep, a bath, and a glass of wine." - Thomas Aquinas

Rose was up early the next morning. She slept well after last night's decision and loved having a plan and working toward executing it. She allowed herself to take a nice warm bath before she headed to her father's study. They all called it his study, but the room was all decked out as a proper office with a big desk, filing cabinets, a copy machine, and various other business machines and supplies. Nestled amongst the papers and growing guides on the bookshelf behind the desk she saw some pictures her father had always kept there. There were many pictures of her and Lea running through the vineyard. Memories of fun times with Lea seeped back into her memory and she made a conscious decision to try and use more tact with her sister...and try not to loathe her too.

The decision to keep the winery operable had washed a lot of her negative feelings for her sister away. She was ready to roll up her sleeves, dive into her father's papers, and make this venture work. She knew she might have to hire help for Manuel. She might need another vintner to help run things as she had her own career to think of. Rose contacted her law office and received permission for one additional week of bereavement in which to settle her father's affairs.

Isobel had found Rose deep in concentration and brought her fresh coffee, a small plate of freshly picked fruit, and a pan dulce...a sweet bread. Isobel remembered how Alain was dedicated to his work and saw the same qualities in Rose.

    Lea slept about an hour longer than her sister. Once awake, she lay in bed for a while playing games on her cell phone before dragging herself out of bed and throwing on shorts and a light cotton blouse. She wasn't a robe-wearing gal like her sister, she thought to herself. Lea felt it was always better to be ready in case you needed to go somewhere. She had always been a bit more of a tomboy than her sister who had to primp, preen, and dress well as an attorney. Rose was always more careful about everything including her looks, she thought. Lea also thought this was silly of Rose as she always looked pretty no matter if she was in a robe or dressed for court or even a night out.

    She wanted to get some coffee and made her way downstairs. She found Isobel singing and cooking in the kitchen as usual. It made her feel warm to have some things remain as they always have been. Isobel could never replace their mother, but she had watched the girls grow up and she was a surrogate mother of sorts, or like a close aunt.

    "Good morning, Isobel!"
Isobel turned from the sink quickly and glanced at Lea before turning back to her work and responding; "Buenos Dias Lea. Would you like some breakfast?"

Lea walked over to the sink to see Isobel washing vegetables for a later meal. "No thanks. I'm not very hungry."

"But you have not eaten much since before the funeral. You must keep up your strength."

"You're probably right, but I'm really not hungry. Maybe I need a little walk to get my appetite going?"

"That sounds good mi hija. And when you come back, I will make you whatever you like, okay?"

"Thank you, Isobel. That sounds wonderful" she said and hugged Isobel tightly before leaving the kitchen to go out on the back patio. Outside the sun was already hanging brightly over the vineyard and a reflective shimmering of light could be seen from the glassy skin of the hanging grapes, which were near their harvest time. Lea spied Manuel way out at the far end of the vineyard. She decided it would make a good walk to go out to see him. Although the sun was up, the air was still cool and a light breeze was blowing. The breeze was not enough to make her feel cold as she made the long walk to the end of the vineyard while the sun-drenched her in warmth.

"Good morning, Manuel!" Manuel had noticed her approach as he worked checking the grapes. "Good morning Little One. How are you today?"

"Much better thanks. The funeral was tough, but I'm trying to get back to normal. I miss Mom and

39

Dad so much and it will always hurt, but I just can't lay in bed anymore. I feel so useless. I know Rose is working on Dad's papers and you and Isobel are always so busy taking care of things. I just thought it was time I got up." Manuel was silent for a full minute before replying. Lea was used to this with him. She knew he usually took time to get his thoughts in order and translate them into spoken English. Manuel was always judicious with his words and also wise whenever he did choose to speak.

"Little One, it is good to mourn and it is good to work. Work reminds us that we are alive and how better to honor the memory of our departed loved ones than by continuing with our work…with living. You are finding a balance. Never forget your parents, but also do not neglect yourself." Manuel kept checking grapes up and down the aisles as Lea followed him just as she did when she was a little girl. After a few minutes, Lea spoke again.

"Can I help you today?'

"Of course, my Dear! Follow me." Lea knew Manuel had spent the last six months pruning the vines, tilling the soil, and planting new vines as needed. Manuel walked her over to a row that had not been tended to yet and instructed her to tie the vine shoots to the trellis system. She had done this many times before as an adolescent and teen and had no problem getting started and moving down the row quickly. She was almost as quick as Manuel and was almost able to match his pace of work. Time amongst the vines always passed quickly and allowed one to let their thoughts wander.

Manuel always understood it was best to let Rose work in silence and wait for her to share her thoughts when she was ready. Although he maintained what outwardly appeared to be a humble innocence that some mistook for 'simple,' he was a deep thinker and wise. He had little formal education in Mexico, but once he learned English, he became an avid reader and Alain had often loaned him books and together they would sit on the back porch discussing them over wine. He knew Rose would speak when she was ready and after some considerable time, she did.

"Manuel, I know I can count on you and Isobel, but do you feel I am making the right decision?"

"First, you must remember the decision was not yours alone. Your sister has committed to it too. Now…what I think does not matter as much as what you girls think, but I think your father would want you to continue. Whether you succeed or not is left to be seen, but I feel you both have made the right decision for now. That might not help, but continuing your parents' goals, at least for now, is certainly a noble decision."

"Thanks Manuel. I needed to hear that."

He gave her a quick smile as they both continued working in silence.

Several hours had passed before she knew it as Isobel called them to come to the patio for lunch.

Rose had spent the morning familiarizing herself with all the bills, invoices, money going out, money trickling in, various expenses, and so much more. Her mind was swimming from all the sundry details and she could feel a migraine coming on as Isobel knocked on the office door and announced lunch was ready on the patio. Still, in her robe, she made her way downstairs and outside, joining the others for lunch. Few words passed between them as they ate. Isobel finally asked Rose how her research into their business affairs was going.

"Oh gosh. There is so much to go over. It seems like so much money goes out, but very little comes in. I'm not sure how Dad kept this all running. I'm still trying to make sense of it all." Rose did not dare mention she now knew just how much Manuel and Isobel were making in salary and was a bit bewildered at how much her father paid them. She knew they were probably worth every penny they were paid, but with the small amount of income over the last few years, based on wine sales, it seemed her father kept them on even though he was bleeding money.

"Isobel, do you have any idea how Dad managed to make ends meet with the winery? It seems like he has been in-the-red a lot these last few years."

"Hmm…not really mi hija. Things have been tight, but we always made things work. Manuel and I always did our part to help keep Alain's dream alive. Your father really believed in making a great wine people would enjoy. He was always trying new things to improve the soil, the grapes, and so on. As you know, these vines," she said as she swept her arm across the vineyard, "are laced with his blood, his sweat, and his tears. I know I sound a bit dramatic, but it is the truth. Manuel and I loved both of your parents…we love you girls…and have never forgotten all that your parents did to help us establish ourselves here in this country. All we have, we shared with your parents."

Manuel added, *"El destino se trata de buscar y encontrar formas de servir a los demás."* The girls both looked at him and it was Rose who spoke first.

"What does that mean? My Spanish is not that good, but it sounds like you mentioned something about destiny?"

Manuel smiled and said, "Yes. I was paraphrasing from a quote I read in one of the books your father let me borrow. It was from a man named Albert Schweitzer who believed in what he called a 'Reverence for Life.' It means destiny is about seeking and finding ways to serve others. Isobel and I love serving your family. Your father loved serving others by making good wine and helping others when he could. You two will now have to find your destinies."

Rose, ever the practical one replied, "I understand we need to make a decision Manuel, but we may be severely handicapped in keeping the winery operating without enough money coming in. It would be great to find our destinies, but our destinies may be limited to what we can afford." Both Isobel and Manuel looked at each other and smiled as Manuel said, "Where there is love, there will be a way."

"Is that another famous quote Manuel?" Lea asked.

"No Little One. Not famous. It is just from my heart to your ears. Pray and think and a way will become clear."

After lunch, Rose went back to the study. She thought about Isobel and Manuel and how much she loved them, but also felt they were simple people. How could prayer pay these bills? She needed to continue looking through her father's records and hoped an answer would emerge before she might be forced to make some tough decisions. Isobel cleared the patio table and did the dishes as Lea and Manuel returned to the vineyard to continue tying the vines to the trellis system. Just as Lea was finishing the last of the tying, her cell phone rang and she answered it.

"Oh Lea, this is Roxy. I wanted to check up on you and see how you were holding up. I'm sure it's been tough on you. How are you coping?"

"Thanks for checking on me. It's getting better. We held the funeral and my sister and I have decided to keep the winery going."

"But, I thought you two didn't get along?"

"We don't. We've had some heated words already, but I think we are both going to try and work together."

Lea and Roxy talked for a while before Roxy suggested coming out to the winery for a 'cheer up' visit as she called it. Lea said it would be nice to see her and mentioned that she had no plans for tonight. They decided to order a pizza and open a bottle of wine and just have some girl-talk time, which Lea was really looking forward to. This would be a nice respite from all the grief and mourning. Lea let Isobel know she had a friend coming to visit and would not be joining them for dinner as she and her friend would take their pizza and hang out in the barn.

Roxy arrived just after 7 PM and the girls made their way straight out to the barn. The barn had enough room for a crusher-destemmer machine, a controlled pressure wine press, various tanks, and oak barrels, as well as the cases of empty bottles waiting to be filled and the filled bottles waiting to be distributed. Roxy had never been to the barn before and was impressed. The girls sat at a small table and ate pizza, drank a bottle of Chateau Baudin cabernet, and talked about life and friends. Roxy's visit helped Lea feel normal again after the last few days of grieving. The two had met just prior to sharing a dorm at San Diego State University where they took a few classes together. Roxy said she was a true bohemian who devoted herself to fun and art, in that order. She was a

45

fun, vibrant person and Lea always enjoyed hanging out with such a free spirit as she saw herself. Lea felt great catching up on the gossip as if it were nourishment after a long fast. This time it was Roxy's cell phone that rang.

"Hello?...Oh hey! I'm visiting my friend Lea in Temecula right now. Really?! Do you really want to leave them? Cool...Let me check with Lea." Roxy put her phone on mute before addressing Lea.

"Oh my gosh! You'll never guess, but Colin Bannerman, only the cutest guy at State, is in Old Town Temecula right now with some friends! They all drove up for line dancing at some country bar, but he wants to ditch them and hang out with us. He says he hates country dancing. He's more of the rocker type. What do you think? Are you cool with him coming over?"

Lea didn't really think about it before responding. She just shrugged her shoulders and said, "Sure, he can come over."

Roxy's smile grew even larger than normal as she unmuted her phone and relayed the news to Colin and gave him the address. Lea knew he would be over soon so the girls went to the front of the winery to meet him. Within twenty minutes Colin arrived on his motorcycle, parked, and removed his helmet. Lea was instantly taken by Colin's bright blue eyes, his thick wavy dark brown hair, and his tall, thin, lanky build. Roxy introduced them and the three of them went back out to the barn to share a second bottle of wine and hang out.

    Colin was friendly and talked easily on many subjects and also knew just what to say to make the girls laugh. Although Lea had not been too excited about Roxy inviting this guy over, she was starting to appreciate how he livened up her mood. Lea found herself enjoying his laid-back attitude. She felt like she could relate to him. He seemed like another free spirit like Roxy and herself. For instance, when politics was mentioned, he told them, "Why bother voting? No matter who you vote for, the government still wins." Or when money was brought up, he said, "I feel the retirement system should be flipped around so you can party and enjoy life with a monthly pension when you are young and finally go to work when you reach retirement age. Think about it. When you reach an age where you can retire, you don't want to do anything anymore anyway. All the retired people I know just sit around eating and watching television instead of living life. Why not go to work then instead of when you are young and want to do things?" Lea realized some of his thinking was ridiculous, but she admired his confidence and his thinking there must be other ways to live than just conforming to the norm. After starting on their third bottle of wine, Lea mentioned she was starting to feel cold.

    Colin smiled at her and said, "I can make us a small bonfire." Lea kept talking to Roxy and did not pay attention to Colin. Colin and his friends often enjoyed ring fires at the beach and figured a barrel would work just fine. He had seen people use barrels before and there were so many in the barn. He selected one and dragged it near the girls and filled it with whatever he could find, old packing material, discarded paper on a small table, some scraps of wood, and so on. He then took out his lighter and lit the material on fire. He had a nice little fire going in no time and as he stood over the barrel with his outstretched hands getting warm, he told the girls to move their chairs over to enjoy the warmth.

    Rose had spent all day going over her father's business paperwork. She did not learn too much other than the winery had been making a profit until the last couple of years and her father had been keeping the winery going mainly through savings from the past profits. She was glad to find out he did not seem to have any big loans out, just a few small ones for various equipment he had to purchase. That was a relief as a big loan might tilt the decision toward selling off the winery.

    As she worked, she thought about how much she loved her parents. Even though she had not been around much to visit over the last few years, she had a happy childhood filled with warmth, love, and adventure among the family vines. She was glad her parents raised her to enjoy the outdoors. She also had great role models on the benefits of keeping a strong work ethic. She realized that while the vineyard had been her grandfather's dream and then her parents' dream to turn it into a commercial winery and it had never been her or her sister's dream, she felt an obligation to continue their legacy beyond merely obligation. She did have love for the vines and the home her family had built up. Each family member had put their mark, so to speak, on this inheritance and she was now becoming resolved to make her mark too, if she could pull it off.

After all the hours she spent, Rose made some personal decisions. She felt she owed it to her grandparents, her parents, and even to Isobel and Manuel to try and make a go of keeping the winery open and making it successful again. She figured Lea would not care either way. She tried not to have a low opinion of her sister, but Lea tended to act in ways that Rose found flaky. She thought back to their childhood and remembered all the countless times Lea was late to an event, missed deadlines with homework, forgot to do something, and so on. In her eyes, Lea always acted about everything as if she didn't care even though she was nice and respectful to people, but just a flake. Rose decided she would have to put her law career on hold to keep her family's dream alive. But was Lea right? Was it her dream too? She decided to go with her gut feeling, which told her to not let the winery fail.

She had spent so many hours in the study, that she even fell asleep face down on her father's desk for a while. When she awoke, she decided she should just go to bed, but maybe have a bath first. She left the study and went downstairs to pour herself a big glass of chardonnay. No one was around as it was late so she figured they all had gone to bed. She went back upstairs and ran a bath for herself. She sat on the rim of the tub watching it fill up with warm water as she sipped her wine. Since she knew she was going to run the winery she reasoned that maybe she could get her sister to fall in with her and pitch in. She knew Lea loved their parents too and maybe she could get her to work to help keep the winery open as it would benefit all of them. Rose's optimism was sometimes her downfall, but she had to cling to the idea that with everyone pitching in they could rescue the winery from financial ruin.

When the tub finished filling, she stood up and turned to disrobe. She happened to face the window and saw a fire in the barn! "What the Hell!" she exclaimed before re-robing and running downstairs and out to the barn. What she saw enraged her.

"What the Hell is going on here? I thought the barn was on fire!"
The three friends looked at Rose and Lea quickly tried to defuse the situation. "Rose, chill out. Nothing is happening. My friends and I are just hanging out and Colin made us a bonfire to keep warm."

Rose shouted at Lea, "Chill out!? You can't have a fire inside a wood barn! What are you thinking? Put that out immediately!"

"Hey, no worries. I had it safely contained. The roof is high and I kept the fire away from walls and stuff. I'll put it out." said Colin as he grabbed a nearby fire extinguisher and doused the barrel fire.

Rose turned her attention to Colin and addressed him, "I have no idea who you are and I don't give a shit how safe you think you are. Get out of here! All of you!" She was so angry she was red in the face and shaking. Roxy and Colin made motions to leave, but Lea stopped them and addressed Rose, "You have no right to kick my friends out. If I want friends over, I can have friends over. This is my home too. This winery has been left to both of us."

"Really Lea, you think you are an equal partner here? I've been studying Dad's business all day long while you sit around 'hanging out' with friends drinking up our wine profits. What do you do to help keep us afloat?"

"I spent all day helping Manuel tie up vines to trellises. I care about the winery too! I don't see what is so wrong with having some friends over after a hard day's work?"

Rose started to laugh and said, "You don't see what's wrong?" She pointed to the new oak barrel that was now scorched black on the inside and said, "Look at that barrel. Do you see that?! That was a brand new

51

Tonnellerie O oak wine barrel that cost a thousand dollars. I saw the receipt today, and it's now ruined. That was for our wine and now it's worthless. You just cost us a thousand dollars and if you had caught the barn on fire, it would have been…everything! We also have to pay to have someone refill our extinguisher now too! Why are you so damn blind to your flakiness?!"

"Stop…" was all Lea could say through her tears as she ran out of the barn with Roxy and Colin in tow. She stood in the middle of the vineyard and cried as Roxy tried to console her. Colin stood just outside the barn and lit up a cigarette. Rose made sure the fire was out and walked out of the barn and stood near Colin, but with her eyes on Lea and Roxy. Colin turned toward Rose and said, "Don't you think you're a little hard on her?" Rose flashed angry eyes at him and told him off before storming back into the house. When Lea stopped crying, Roxy and Colin said their goodbyes and left. Lea wandered back into the house where she found Rose sitting at the kitchen table. Rose was sitting at the table with a defeated look on her face, just staring at the wall. Lea sat down across from Rose and they both sat silent for a few minutes. Their eyes had not met as they both just looked at the table in front of them. After a while, it was Lea who spoke first.

"Look Rose, I'm really sorry. I wasn't paying attention and did not realize what Colin was doing at first. We were just cold and he was trying to be nice."

"Nice? That guy seems like an aloof asshole. Do you realize how close we may be to losing the winery? Even a thousand-dollar setback could really hurt us right now."

"Rose, I had no idea, really. I'll pay for a new barrel out of my own savings. Are we really that close to losing the winery?"

"Yes. We can get through one more so-so year, but if we don't get back to making a profit again by next year, we will be in a lot of trouble. I've decided to take a leave of absence to get things going around here."

"Rose, I know you think of me as your little flaky sister. You just said as much, but the truth is I want to help. Our family has worked hard to make this winery and I want to do my part too. I've been aimless and lacking a purpose, but I really do want to do whatever I can to keep our family business going. I don't want us to sell the winery. Let's make a go of it. Working together, maybe we can turn things around."

Rose looked up and met Lea's eyes. She knew her sister might be flaky, but she was always honest. She thought Lea must really want to help and if that is the case, maybe they can turn things around. "Lea, I...we...could really use your help. You are a part of this as much as I am, but I need you to ta..." She was going to say 'take things seriously,' but felt she had hammered Lea enough for now, especially if she was genuinely eager to work as a team...as sisters. What

53

she said instead was, "I need you to take a bath and go to bed. We have a lot of work to do tomorrow and we will need to get up early." She finished by smiling at her sister. Lea returned the smile before getting up and rushing over to Rose's side to give her a great hug.

Lea went to her room, deciding to take a shower in the morning to help wake her up since she was setting her alarm to get up early to tackle whatever needed to be done to save the family concern. Rose returned to her now cold bath. She emptied it, refilled it with hot water, and lit some candles. In her mind, the candles were a silent prayer for household harmony and future success. She was a practical person, but she was also plagued with frequent optimism in her ability to handle risky situations, including her sister. She sat in the warm bath sipping her wine and tried to drain her mind of all thoughts and succumb to relaxation.

Chapter Five

"I drank to drown my pain, but the damned pain learned how to swim..." - Frida Kahlo

Rose called her law office and told them she would need an extended leave of absence. She knew they were extremely reluctant and a bit peeved, but relented as they did not want to lose her. She promised them she just needed to get things sorted out. She related how she wanted to work the first harvest to ensure all would run smoothly without her so she could return to the firm. She used her law skills to plead her case and won herself an extended leave, but at more cost to her personal savings as it would be an unpaid leave.

For several weeks the sisters spent long hours going over paperwork, making repairs, deciding on business strategies, and learning the intricacies of winemaking from Manuel. Harvest time was quickly approaching and Manuel explained to the sisters that they harvest between the last week of August or within the first two weeks of September, depending on various factors. Manuel told them this time frame is essential to ensure their wines have what he referred to as "refreshing acidity" when the grapes are between a 3 and 4 on a pH scale of acidity.

While both girls handled a lot of the physical work, Rose was the only one who handled the paperwork and business end of things. The sisters had grown up on the winery and realized just how much they knew from the osmosis effect of a childhood spent amongst the vines. They understood their father, Alain, had started using the pyramid stacking of wine barrels, one on top of another with wooden wedges to keep them in place for stacking them three levels high to maximize the little amount of storage space they had in the barn cellar. The barn cellar had been dug by their father and maintained just the right temperature and humidity conducive for wine storage. Alain had spent decades purchasing equipment and making improvements to the point where the sisters would need to buy very little other than new bottles and corks. Many wineries had changed over from using corks, but being French, Alain had insisted they always use corks with the Baudin name imprinted on each. Rose quickly realized their greatest expense would be payroll, not just for Isobel and Manuel, but also for the pickers and assorted part-time help they paid each year to help in wine-making. Luckily, they still had plenty of stock on hand from the last two years to sell while making new wine.

  Rose realized one of their downfalls was that they did not have enough property for a tasting room and gift shop. Most of the local Temecula Valley wineries had elaborate facilities which brought in a lot of ready cash from tourists and wine enthusiasts who wanted to try various wines and maybe enjoy lunch in vineyard surroundings. The family ranch house did have a connected two-car garage and she entertained the idea of converting it into a tasting room in which they could also sell bottles directly. Rose knew this would take a lot of refurbishing and permits but would be doable. She made a mental note to discuss this with Manuel tonight.

In the barn, Lea and Manuel were inspecting and cleaning the equipment in anticipation of the upcoming harvest. Lea was using a pressure hose to wash out their crusher-destemmer while Manuel was inspecting the wine press and tanks. The barn floor was poured concrete with good drainage so they were able to do washes without taking the equipment outside. Lea had taken up the rubber matting which covered the concrete floor so the excess water could better flow to the drains. She didn't realize how slippery the wet concrete was until Manuel climbed down from cleaning out a tall tank and promptly slipped and landed on some equipment that Lea had not put away.

Manuel screamed in pain and was unable to get up. Lea rushed over to help him stand, but he was unable to get up and screamed in pain each time he tried. Lea took off her cleaning gloves and reached for the cell phone in her back pocket. She called 911 emergency first and then called up at the house phone to let the others know Manuel was hurt. As they waited, Lea said from behind tears, "I am so sorry Manuel. It's my fault. I took up the mats."

"No Lea. I saw you were taking them up and I knew you were doing it for the water to drain. I thought it was a good idea too at the time. Please don't worry. People slip and fall all the time. I probably just hit a nerve and I'll be fine in no time. It just hurts to move right now."

"You just lay there until help arrives. Try not to move so you don't cause yourself any further injury."

"Si, mi hija." He mumbled as he grimaced in pain.

The ambulance arrived and carefully got Manuel onto a stretcher and drove off to the hospital. His wife, Isobel, had run down to the barn earlier and held her husband's hand until they picked him up. She went with him in the ambulance. Isobel was scared for Manuel, and inwardly scared for herself if she were to lose him. He had been her rock…her support…her best friend and lover for so long, she could not imagine what life would be like without him. She held his hand and gently stroked his head as the ambulance rushed on.

After the frenzy of getting to the hospital and waiting to be seen, they finally received some answers. X-Rays showed that Manuel had a fractured vertebrae and had pinched some nerves in his back. The doctors would not give a prognosis on his condition until they knew more. They needed to observe him for a few days to determine the extent of the damage and if he could handle physical therapy or needed surgery. Both Rose and Lea had followed the ambulance so they were on hand to comfort Isobel. After a few hours of tests and checks by specialists, Manuel's doctor told the ladies that they could eventually transport him back home so he could recuperate in his own bed, but not for a few days.

They all knew he was certainly in no condition to help with this year's harvest. The sisters were especially worried about Manuel because not only was he sort of a surrogate father now, but he was also a hard worker who often did more than his share with each harvest. He knew the vines. He knew winemaking. It was in his blood much more than in the sisters' blood. Also, Lea was secretly glad Rose did not know she was supposed to be the one to pick up the mats as her sister would have blamed her for Manuel's injuries.

"Rose, what are we going to do if Manuel can no longer work? Will it even be possible for us to complete the harvest? Lea said nervously.

With a hint of exasperation in her face because Lea was forcing her to confront the issue, Rose replied, "We'll do what we always do. We'll figure something out." Rose always kept a 'can do' attitude, but she wondered how much a set-back like this would cost. It could shatter their attempt to keep the winery as a viable operation. Rose walked away as she needed to think by herself.

    With Manuel unable to help, Rose and Lea held fears this year's harvest would be unsuccessful or the wine would be substandard. For a small winery like theirs, this could mean the difference between keeping their doors open or being forced to admit defeat and sell off everything. As Rose sat in her father's office, now her office, she pondered all the possible ramifications and scenarios. Without thinking, she automatically started going through the accumulated stack of mail. One large envelope had a flier for an upcoming wine competition for Temecula Valley wineries. The first prize was a trophy, but also a five-thousand-dollar prize.

    Reading over the details, Rose saw that the Chateau Baudin Winery would have to supply three cases of wine for judging and sampling and they would also have to pay a five-hundred-dollar entry fee. This fee would cover publicity and also be applied toward the prize money. This competition was a long shot, but it could mean a lot of press for them, which would translate to selling bottles. And what if they did win? They could really use the extra money and although they were a small batch winery, people loved the taste of their family wine.

    Wine drinkers were still discovering their wines all the time and sales had been increasing until the opening of the new, bigger wineries a few years back which increased competition for sales, driving their sales down. Chateau Baudin Winery could never supply the sheer quantity the large suppliers demanded. Maybe, if they did win the prize money, they could expand their output somehow or at least fund the creation of their tasting room. She stopped her daydreaming and brought her attention back to the present and how they would handle the harvest.

Every year they would get a few students of agriculture who wanted harvest internships and they also had some regular volunteers made up mostly of their parent's retired friends and some enthusiastic customers. These people enjoyed just being out amongst the vines and the camaraderie shared with the end-of-harvest dinner party that Isobel always took care of. Depending on how Isobel is holding up, they may just have to have catered sandwiches or pizza instead of a huge authentic Mexican dinner. This would sadden the pickers but may be necessary. Since Manuel was the main contact for the pickers, Rose realized she needed to seek out Isobel and find out where they stood with everything. She found Isobel in her room. It looked as if she had just been praying.

"Isobel, I'm sorry to bother you at a time like this, but can I talk to you for a few minutes about the upcoming harvest and some of my ideas?"

"Of course hija, but this is not 'a time like this.' Manuel is injured, not dead. The doctor says he will recover. It is just that his working days may be over, but he could still supervise."

"Sure…of course. Let's talk in the family room. I'll get us some glasses of wine and meet you there."

Rose entered the family room and handed Isobel, who was sitting on one of the couches, a glass of wine. Rose sat on the adjoining couch and started the conversation.

"How is Manuel? I feel so terrible for him getting hurt."

"Manuel is tough from years of work. He has good muscle strength and a strong constitution. I pray for him to get better and the doctor already says he is getting better. After all the x-rays, tests, and so on, they feel he will get back most of his mobility soon without surgery. He will need to go to some physical therapy and take pills for the pain, but he is alive and he is a fighter. I will pick him up and bring him back home tomorrow."

Rose smiled at her and said, "I am so happy to hear that he is getting better and I also pray he gets back to his normal self as much as possible. If we can do anything to make things more comfortable for him around the house, or anything, just let me know." They both took a sip from their wine glasses before Rose continued.

"Isobel, I'm worried about the upcoming harvest. Do you, by any chance, know if Manuel has a list of volunteers? And will you be up to handling the end of picking meal? Because if you are feeling it may be too difficult at this time, I totally understand and we can look at other options."

"No hija, I will be fine. I cook for us anyway. Cooking for a large group will be fine. I will need to tend to Manuel at times, but I see no reason why I cannot cook the harvest meal. As for Manuel's list, I'm pretty sure he has one. I would bet he already has it full too. I know he mentioned working on it a few weeks back. We can ask him to see it tomorrow."

"Thank you, Isobel. You have no idea how much you have relieved my fears. I was getting worried, but you have made me feel better, as you always do." Still smiling, Rose raised her glass to Isobel and said "Salud!" before taking a sip. Isobel returned the comment and did likewise.

-

During the last few weeks, Lea had been in touch with her friend Roxy. Her friend from San Diego State University was becoming her main connection to the outside world beyond the walls of her family's winery. Although they did not have a chance to see each other in person, they would spend a few hours a week on the phone. Roxy loved to gossip and Lea was always glad to hear news about their circle of friends. Roxy had also mentioned that Colin had asked for Lea's number, but wanted to check with Lea if it was okay to give it to him. Lea consented and Colin also started calling her. He seemed a bit of an outspoken rebel to her and not normally the type of guy she would be interested in, but there was *something* about him. She thought she should at least get to know him a little better. Roxy also vouched for him so he must be alright.

    On their initial phone calls, she was a bit aloof, but gradually she became more interested in him as he told her jokes and about his many experiences traveling on his motorcycle. He had a smooth voice and said things that made her feel comfortable. Lea was actually shocked to realize she was starting to be seriously interested in Colin. She even daydreamed that maybe he would be interested in working at the winery with her, but she realized this would mean a greater commitment and she was not sure if she was ready for that. It had been over a year since she broke up with the last guy she had dated, a laid-back surf instructor she had once hired for her failed venture.

    Colin was persistent and one night talked her into meeting him at a bar in Old Town Temecula. They talked, drank, laughed, and so on until the night was wearing out and Lea knew she had to leave if she was going to get any rest before another day of hard work. She made her excuses to go, but she was hesitant to leave those mysterious brown eyes…that lilting smile…and that infectious laugh of his. Uggh. She realized she was getting smitten by his charms. She would have to leave now before she lost any self-control. She said goodbye, stood up and walked out to her car. Colin followed her out. Lea turned as she reached her car and saw him a few feet behind her.

"Hey, are you stalking me?" she said with a playful smile.

"Not at all. I just wanted to make sure you made it to your car okay. Besides, my bike is parked close by. I hope you had a good time tonight?" He spoke smoothly as he slowly advanced. Lea noticed the moonlight reflecting in his eyes as he drew near.

"Of course, I had a great time. I really needed to get out and away from Rose and the winery for a while. I thank you for tonight. It was just what I needed." She had to look up at Colin's rugged features as he drew ever nearer and stood very close to her.

"Lea, I really enjoyed your company tonight. You are very beautiful." He reached out and gently touched her cheek as their eyes met and locked in place for what seemed an eternity to Lea before he leaned in and kissed her on the lips. His kiss felt strong yet soft at the same time and Lea felt her knees quiver a little. The kiss was quick. Colin pulled back and met her eyes one more time before turning to leave for his bike. Lea watched as he mounted his motorcycle and put on his helmet in what seemed one fluid motion. He started the engine and drove off toward the freeway entrance and back toward San Diego. She kept thinking there was something fascinating about him...his bravado...his swagger. Lea stood frozen for a full second after he was gone, then got in her car and went home with dreams in her head of what her future may bring.

  The next day, Isobel left early to pick up Manuel from the hospital. Rose offered to go and help her with him, but Isobel said she would be fine on her own. Isobel knew Rose had plenty of work to do and also knew Manuel could move enough to get in and out of the car by himself. Rose and Lea tended to the various and sundry everyday things which went into running a winery. They knew the harvest was coming up fast and there was a lot to do to get ready. Rose also told Lea about the competition and they both agreed it would be a good idea.

  While Lea busied herself with getting all the tools and various equipment ready for the pickers, Rose filled out the registration form and paid the five hundred dollars online. She felt a little sting as she paid, but it was an investment in their future. She then went and put aside the three cases she would need to drive over to the competition office. Lea decided she would make tuna sandwiches for all of them for when Isobel and Manuel would return. Just as she finished, she heard a car pull up out front. She yelled to let Rose know and ran out to meet it.

  Manuel was moving slowly and in obvious pain, but he could move on his own. They brought him inside and straight to the kitchen where they had a chair waiting for him with an extra cushion to sit on.

Rose joined them and they enjoyed their sandwiches together while talking about Manuel's back and the treatment he would need and other aspects of his injury.

He would not be able to work for at least two months. This was terrible news to the girls, but they had been prepared to hear as much. As they finished their meal, Rose asked, "Manuel, where can I find your list of the volunteer pickers? I will contact them for you, this year, and Lea and I will both work with them in the vineyard." Manuel averted his eyes from her, as if he had been kicked, and took a minute before he looked at her again with a pained expression and answered, "The list and contacts have been destroyed. We will need to post new notices for help." There was silence for almost a complete minute as a stunned Rose said, "What happened? It will be tough to get volunteers this late in the season."

"I'm sorry Rose. They were on my little work desk in the barn and now they are gone. I feel it is my fault. Your father gave me a laptop, but I didn't know how to use it so I wrote everything down by hand."

"But how…What happened to them?" Manuel looked at Lea briefly before turning back to Rose and said, "I don't want to get anyone in trouble. That is why I have not spoken of this before. I meant to get new volunteers, but then my back…"

Rose, starting to get agitated, demanded, "Tell me what happened to the list."

"They were burned. Burned in that barrel we need to replace." Rose turned sharply to Lea and spoke, "So! This is your fault. That figures. It's not enough you ruin a thousand-dollar barrel, but you also sabotage our chances to get enough pickers for our harvest. Damnit Lea!" Rose was torn between wanting to cry and scream. Lea had had enough of Rose's picking on her and lashed back, "Screw you, Rose! You always play so high and mighty with me, but I never meant for anything to get wrecked...the barrel or the list."

"But it's your fault. You brought those so-called friends here...that biker thug has caused us enough trouble. You were not being responsible and you allowed them to cause destruction to the winery. This is really going to set us back. Keep those friends of yours away from here from now on." Rose spat the words out before standing up and was about to storm off when Lea stopped her by proclaiming, "No Rose. I can have anyone I want visit and I like Colin. We are starting to see each other and if I want to bring him to *my home*, I will." Rose stared at Lea with intense anger before turning and storming out of the kitchen. Lea said to her back, "That's typical of you, Rose. Running off instead of confronting problems."

-

The girls avoided each other all that day and into the next. Rose got up early to avoid Lea and took the three cases of their best chardonnay from last year to the wine competition office. She was told her winery was the last one to enter out of twenty-one that had already signed up. Her boxes were marked with a "22" and she was given paperwork outlining all the rules of the blind tasting and when and where the judging would take place and her tickets to the event. She was still so angry thinking about Lea that she barely heard a word anyone said. She grabbed all the paperwork, turned to leave, and was pushing the door out as someone on the other side pushed the door in, knocking her on her behind and scattering all the papers around. She was furious as she looked up and saw a man about her age with a field worker's tan and cowboy hat coming in with three cases of wine. He put the boxes down so he could see her and their blue eyes met. Rose was about to tell this guy off, but something kept her from it. She would never allow herself to believe it was his rugged good looks, his broad shoulders, or his winsome smile as he said to her, "Damnit gal…you almost made me drop my wine. You gotta watch where you're goin' miss. Here I'll help you up." He reached out a long, muscular arm and practically picked her off the floor with no effort. All Rose could say was, "Yeah…my papers…" and the guy quickly picked up all her scattered papers and handed them back to her. She took them and this guy picked up his cases of wine and left them to be tagged "17" before turning and seeing Rose was still there.

"Oh, you're still here? Well, I'm sorry you got knocked down. Name's Ryan Alexander and I'm with Madame Tautou Winery." he said as he reached his hand out. Rose shook his large, muscular hand and could only say, "No problem. I'm Rose. From Chateau Baudin Winery. Let's not meet like this again, okay?" He smiled at her and said "Okay, Rose" before rushing out the door and leaving. The sunlight pierced the room as the door swung open and bathed a stunned Rose in its warm glow.

Chapter Six

"He who loves not women, wine, and song remains a fool his whole life long." - Martin Luther

The scorching, stifling days under the August sun bled each night into the hot, still evenings every Californian knew. Many residents had swimming pools in which to pass these nights in some cool, refreshing semblance of comfort, and the poolside wines, which flowed freely, were always a big part of that comfort. Rose never thought much about the romanticized side of wine drinking, but to Lea, it was this *joie de vivre* which mattered most in why anyone should even bother making a worthy wine. Rose was both sentimental and practical. She wanted her family's winery to succeed because she loved her parents and knew it was their only and necessary income.

Rose and Lea avoided each other for the last few days of August. Both girls had an inert stubbornness they inherited as part of both their French and Jewish heritage even though both were innately Californian in their demeanor and personalities. Lea epitomized the laid-back surfer blonde as seen in movies while Rose was the feminist type A personality that the state is known to breed. Being type A, Rose did not let the burned volunteer picker list get her down as she resolved to just put-up flyers all over town asking again for volunteers. She hoped this was just a minor setback. She had a thousand flyers printed up on astro-bright yellow stock paper and went about stapling them up on local telephone poles and various bulletin boards within stores. She would do some online advertising later, but she felt the many wine enthusiasts who flooded the Temecula Valley each weekend would be best reached by flyers they would spot as they drove from winery to winery.

As Rose stapled a flyer to a telephone pole, a beat-up white truck pulled over into the gravel next to her, rolled down the passenger side window, and she heard a voice yell out, "Hey, you know you can't do that, right?" Rose turned toward the voice and saw it was the guy she had met at the competition office, Ryan something.

"Legally, I can. Utility poles are one of the few legal areas where I can post a flyer."

"No, you ninny. I mean you can't use volunteer labor for your harvest. You'll get fined heavily."

Rose walked over to the truck with anger in her voice as she said, "Buzz off creep! We always use volunteers. My father had many people who begged him to come out and help with the harvest. If anyone is a 'ninny' it's you." She crossed her arms awaiting his retort, but she only heard laughter from inside the truck cab. Ryan, when he stopped laughing, said, "Well, I warned you. Check it out for yourself." and he drove off leaving Rose sputtering in the wake of the dust his truck kicked up from the gravel. She muttered, "Asshole." under her breath and decided to head home for lunch. As she drove home in anger, she did decide to check the veracity of Ryan somethings claim so she could be the one to laugh in his face the next time they met.

Unfortunately, she found the laws had changed a few years back and Ryan was correct. It was easy to look up the labor laws in California with a quick search on the internet. The winery could not use volunteer labor which meant yet another setback for them as they would have to pay for workers. Worse yet, they would also have to carry workers' compensation insurance. Shit, she thought. Shit, shit, shit. There was no way Chateau Baudin Winery could afford that.

She immediately sought out Manuel for his insight. She found both Manuel and Isobel in their room. Manuel was lying in bed, propped up by big pillows while Isobel was trying to feed him. The door was open, but she knocked anyway, out of respect, and was welcomed to enter. The older couple was used to Rose's abruptness and she did not disappoint them.

"Guys...Isobel, Manuel...I have to ask you something..." Rose caught herself and knew she should ask about Manuel's health, "Er...how are you, Manuel? Feeling any better?"

"Yes Rose, my dear, I am fine. Every day I am starting to feel better. What can we do for you?"

"Well, you know how the volunteer list and their contact info were burned?"

"Yes…"

"Did my father use volunteers last year?"

"Yes, dear. He used volunteers every year. Almost the exact same people every year. I would call them fans of the winery. Many nice people. Some are doctors and even a few lawyers like yourself." Manuel smiled at her, proud to think of the harvest crew they had every year.

"Uhmm…did Dad know the law had changed? Did he know he legally could not use volunteers anymore?"

Manuel started to laugh, but it turned into a cough and a pained look on his face. It took him a full minute before he could answer, "Yes, but he paid each worker one dollar to get around that."

"But that was not legal."

"The people who came each year loved to help with the harvest. There was even one heart surgeon who made a quarter-million a year, yet he still came each year to harvest for a dollar. The people who come here love to help. They loved the wine. They loved being connected to the earth and the fieldwork. They did not care about the money and they did not complain."

"I get that, but we can't do that anymore. One winery was fined so heavily that they went out of business. We will need to hire workers at minimum

74

wage, but we also need to carry worker's compensation insurance. I don't think we can afford all of that. This will be very tough for us."

Manuel looked at his Isobel and they smiled at each other before they looked at Rose and Isobel said, "The Lord will provide, hija. Have no fear. There is a part in the Bible that says if you choose to work hard and keep your head down, others will follow your lead. We know things will work out."

Rose, while she respected Isobel and Manuel, often got annoyed by their simplistic views on life, said "I hope you are right." and left the room. She went back to her office, shut the door, sat down, and banged her head on the desk. She stayed there, with her head on the desk, thinking about how she could get past this hurdle. Another challenge to test her. She wanted to cry, but she was too strong for that. She was too busy trying to think herself out of this newest puzzle when the phone on her desk rang. She lifted herself up and picked up the receiver after the third ring.

"Hello, Chateau Baudin Winery. How may I help you?" She tried to sound as professional as her emotions would allow.

"Hey Ninny, this is Ryan Alexander. Did you check out the laws like I told you?'

Rose's nostrils flared in anger, but she calmed herself down. He had been right after all.

"Yes, and you were right. I can't use volunteers. Thanks for calling." She started to lower the receiver to hang up, but she heard him talking loudly, "Hey! Hang on, you. I'm calling to offer some help." She put the phone to her ear again and said, "I'm listening."

"Look, you can't have volunteers, but you can have interns. Even though I work for the Tautou winery, I'm allowed to take other jobs after we're done with our harvest. There are not enough pickers for all the wineries, so my boss doesn't mind if we hire ourselves out…after we have picked all their grapes first, of course. You would have to enlist my friends and I as interns and train us in something to do with winemaking to get around the laws, but we can make it work."

"Why would you want to help me? I'm a ninny, remember?" said Rose incredulously.

"Well, let's say I root for the underdog."

"Are you calling me a dog now too?'

"Calm down. I knew your father. I respected him. He always gave of himself and shared what he knew…or even just had time to talk or give his advice. I respected him and I'm sad he's gone. He was a real vintner and a gentleman too. He helped me get over being a reckless youth and got me the job at Madame Tautou. I would be honored to help you bring in your harvest."

Rose, overcome by emotion, said "Call back tomorrow." She hung up the phone and laid her head down on her father's desk and cried. She cried because she missed her father. She cried because she was scared of running a vineyard. She cried because she felt she was giving up her law career out of sentimentality. She cried because she did not know what else to do.

-

Lea had spent the day in San Diego hanging out with Colin Bannerman. Colin seemed a bit wild and feral in her eyes and she was attracted to his bad-boy image like a moth to a flame. She had mostly known laid-back guys, like herself, but Colin was brooding and intense. Colin was a whirlwind. He took her to the Lucha Libre Taco Shop where they sat in 'the ring' and enjoyed amazing tacos and salsa while dressed in Mexican wrestler gear and screaming gritas into a microphone. Afterward, he took her on his motorcycle to the San Diego Zoo where he doted on Lea. She felt lucky to be with such a cool guy who seemed so interested in her. They ended their evening next to a bonfire on the beach in Mission Bay. As the night wore on, they talked about life, the universe, and everything. They finally shared intimate kisses beside their beach bonfire and declared themselves to each other. They were now officially dating. To hell with Rose, thought Lea. She would just have to get to know Colin and see for herself what a great guy he is. Although Lea was smitten, she made it home and went to bed.

The next morning the girls were called to an early breakfast by Isobel. Lea and Rose sat at the table as Isobel put the food down in front of them and said, "Today I made moyettes and chilaquiles. Enjoy. I must go and take a plate to Manuel." The food looked amazing as ever and the girls knew they were in for a treat. Isobel left the kitchen with a tray of food and the girls were alone together for the first time in days. Neither of the girls spoke for quite a while, but finally, Lea gathered enough courage to blurt out, "I'm officially dating Colin now. We have met a few times and he's really cool and sweet and I may even invite him to visit soon."

Rose measured her words carefully before replying, "If you are sure about him, I will try to get to know him, but keep him away from our barrels."

Lea put down her fork and looked at her sister. "Is that all you can say?"

"What more do you want? I'll try to get to know him. That's positive."

"Just be nice to him, Rose. I like him. He's a nice guy."

"He doesn't seem like your usual type. He seems a bit wild."

"You're only basing that on one meeting. You'll like him once you get to know him."

"I hope so."

Lea wondered what her sister was thinking, but gave up dwelling on it and ate her breakfast. Rose did not like the idea of Colin, but she was too busy being concerned about having workers for the harvest. The girls finished breakfast and left the kitchen. Rose was paying bills when the phone rang in the office.

"Hello. Chateau Baudin Winery, how may I help you?"

"Hey Ninny, Ryan here. Are you ready to talk now?"

"Stop calling me that. My name is Rose. What do you want?"

"Okay...Rose, you told me to call back today. Are you ready to talk about how you can hire my friends and I to bring in your harvest?"

"Okay. What can you do to help me?" Rose listened as Ryan outlined his plan. It made sense. She listened and grudgingly agreed to what Ryan Alexander proposed. Being a shrewd lawyer, she thought she might deflect his message as pure bullshit, but he made sense. She was compelled to listen to his ideas and they, surprisingly to her, made sense. She had a plan now and it was thanks to a guy who had knocked her on her butt and had called her, a practicing New York attorney, a ninny. He was handsome, she thought, but what a goofball. He was obviously uneducated, she reasoned. Handsome, but just a field hand she thought. She could never be interested in a low life like him. Ryan did make good sense on the phone and she did need help with the harvest. She agreed to Ryan's plan, got off the phone, and channeled her energy into the upcoming wine competition.

Even though the beginning of September is the time for the grape harvest, and the busiest time for local vineyards. The annual wine judging of local wines was always held on the third weekend of September to appease the tourists and wine enthusiasts who had spent all summer pouring the results into their mouths and immediately after harvest was over for the wineries so they could use the competition to have fun after all their hard work. This year, the judging will be for twenty-two wineries. Alain never entered the Baudin wines for many reasons. Although he thought his wines were superior to most, he also distrusted the judging as the larger wineries usually won. In his mind he figured bribery was the reason, so he never entered the competition. Rose was taking a big chance, but she felt it was just the thing to do. She reasoned that if they won, it could help a lot, and losing couldn't hurt them any more than how they were now.

As August ended and September began, Rose busied herself taking Brix readings on a refractometer to check for sugar levels in the grapes. Her father had taught her how to check what he said was 'the phenolic ripeness' by sampling grapes right on the vine to check if grape skins lost their bitter flavor and that these skins had softened and sweetened. Rose remembered her father would say things to her like, "A big soft, fat, and lazy grape will make a sweet and balanced wine. Bitter fruit only makes for a bitter wine." Although she took daily readings early before the sun's rays touched their vines, the rest of her day was taken up with bookkeeping and ordering supplies like more bottles, corks, and the necessary amount of yeast for fermentation. She also grudgingly ordered a new barrel to replace the burnt one.

During this time, Lea double-checked to make sure all the pickers' gear was clean and ready to be used. She also made sure all their tanks were emptied out and any last amounts of wine were quickly bottled. Lea then washed and tested all equipment. Her mother had always reminded her, "Just as a house must be clean, so must all the tools used to make wine to ensure the purest flavor, free from contaminants." She never minded doing the more physical work and often thought how glad she was Rose handled anything with numbers such as the pH readings, accounting, payroll, and so on.

As the first weekend of September passed, everyone remained calm. Rose had shared the details regarding how Ryan would do the harvest and all felt it was a good plan. By the second weekend in September, they were starting to get nervous as the prime picking time was drawing to a close. Grapes left too long on the vine get sweeter as their sugar levels go up, but they lose their acidity and the tannins necessary to make good wine. Rose's readings showed they would be fine if picked very soon, but she knew they could not wait much longer. Fortunately for all, Ryan called late on Sunday night and told them he and his crew would be there on Tuesday at 3 AM to start picking. Rose felt that would be alright and the grapes should be okay until then. That Monday for all of them was tough. A day of waiting, like an expectant father awaiting news on his newborn offspring. They were all worried. Manuel even said he was feeling better and might start picking that evening to get a jump start, but everyone talked him out of it. It was evident he was physically not yet up to picking. Monday passed too slowly for all at Chateau Baudin Winery and they could barely sleep that evening even though they knew the men would be there early to start the harvesting.

    Rose got up at 2 AM and went into the vineyard with her refractometer and a flashlight to make final readings. Everything looked good. She went back inside and grabbed various snacks and drinks, which she placed out on the back patio for the men, and then she sat down and waited. 3 AM and no one had arrived. She tried to stay calm, but she started biting her nails. 3:15 AM and still nobody. Her nervousness was increasing. She tried not to think bad thoughts, but they would creep back into her mind. 3:30 AM and still no sign of the men. She tried calling Ryan, but his phone kept going to voicemail and the message box was full so she could not even leave a message. Her eyes were starting to water as Isobel came out, sat next to her, and put her arm around Rose, saying nothing. Lea came out back, yawned and stretched, and sat down too. The pregnant silence was not broken until Manuel, who was propped up in his recliner upstairs facing his window, yelled out, "I see three trucks coming this way!" Ryan and his men had arrived. Rose's sadness turned to vexed agitation, but she kept her mouth shut as she could not afford to lose these workers because of something terrible she may say.

    The trucks had parked and the men started piling out. Ryan ran up to Rose and said, "I am so sorry we ran late. A couple of the guys were out partying too late last night and had to be coaxed out of bed and Paul blew a tire on the way over, but we're here now and ready to go." Rose allowed her anger to subside, mumbled "Thank you" and proceeded to give instructions while Lea handed out buckets, gloves, and cutters to any man who needed them. Ryan made sure to introduce himself to Lea before he turned toward the vines with his men and the harvest was officially underway. With a team of nine men, Rose, and Lea all picking together, they were done by 11 AM and beat the midday heat as they hoped. Everyone was feeling beat and welcomed the cold beer Isobel provided while awaiting their 'picker's lunch.' Isobel had spent all morning cooking and her food did not disappoint.

She had sizzling platters of various types of meat and vegetables for fajitas, her special beef empanadas, heaping bowls of rice and beans, and much more along with all the cold beer and wine they could drink.

    While the men ate, Rose and Lea were busy running the grapes through the crusher-destemmer before putting them into the wine press to extract all the juice, which was then put into the awaiting wine tanks. Rose and Lea worked smoothly together like a well-practiced team. Although they often did not get along, each sister knew their livelihood depended on what they could make off their wine. After the men ate, they started to leave. Soon, Ryan Alexander was the only one left as he went to join the sisters who were working in the barn.

    "Rose…Lea…today went really well. Looks like you had a good yield of grapes."

    Lea smiled warmly and said, "Yes, we think we have around twenty tons of grapes."

    "Really? That much?"

    This time Rose turned away from the wine press and said, "Sure. We have five acres planted. Each acre can produce between three to five tons of grapes so if we average it out to four tons of grapes per acre, then we should have twenty tons. That will translate to about three thousand gallons which should make about one-hundred and eleven thousand bottles." She marveled inwardly at how many more bottles they can produce now than when her grandfather started out making just a few hundred bottles a year.

Ryan cracked a big smile, shaking his head a little before replying, "Rose, you do have a sharp mind. Remind me never to go against you in one of those 'guess how many gumballs are in the jar' competitions."

Rose finally smiled and said, "Oh, you probably want me to settle up on the pay. Hold on a minute."

"No Rose. It's okay. You two are really busy and my guys just got paid from Madame Tautou so they're flush at the moment. Besides, I already told them you would pay us at the wine judging next weekend. So, no worries. Just find me at the competition and we'll settle then. Bye ladies." Ryan tipped his cowboy at the girls and left the barn. Rose was already back to what she was doing, but Lea watched as Ryan strode away through the vineyard toward his car.

"Hey Rose, that Ryan is quite the hunk, huh?"

Rose was deep in concentration on what she was doing and just answered with a grunt.

"Come on Rose. He's cute."

"Who? Oh, Ryan? Yes. He's handsome. Not very bright, but good looking." Rose wanted to add that Ryan would be a better match for her sister than Colin, but she kept her diplomacy intact and her mouth shut. Lea went back to helping Rose with the work, but in her mind, she was thinking a tall, tan, muscular guy like Ryan might be just the type to bring her stodgy sister out of her shell and relax a little. As Ryan drove away, he thought about Rose and was glad he made it so she had to seek him out at the wine judging.

Chapter Seven

"Enjoying fine food and wine at the family table, surrounded by your loved ones and friends, is not just a joy -It's one of the highest forms of living."
- Robert Mondavi

The morning of the wine judging arrived all too quick for Rose and Lea as they worked incessantly to destem, press, and get their grape juice into the awaiting tanks for fermentation. Rose had almost wished she had not entered the competition, but it was too late to back out now. Each year the larger wineries put in bids to host the judging and this year it was settled that Madame Tautou Winery would have the honor. The Madame Tautou Winery was a large-scale winery with lots of free parking, a small on-site restaurant, two tasting rooms, a large banquet hall, and of course the lab area and fermentation tanks. They even had tours of their specially constructed wine cellar which maintained a constant fifty-five degrees. For the judging, most of the public areas would be roped off for participants in the event. A select panel of five judges, made up of sommeliers and oenophiles unconnected to any of the local wineries, would conduct the actual judging this year. Anyone could take part in self-judging the competing wines as long as they paid an extra fee to sample all the varietal wines and blends, otherwise, one tasting room would be left to the general visiting public.

    Rose rushed to get cleaned up and find something a little nicer to wear than the jeans, T-shirts, and flannels she had lately been accustomed to. She caught a glimpse of Lea as she ran past Rose's room and saw she was sporting a pretty yellow summer dress with white gloves, heels, and a hat to match. Lea yelled out, "Try to dress up a bit Rose. Try to be a bit girlie today." With a roll of her eyes and a quick shudder, she controlled her anger as Lea had always taunted her about her tomboyishness growing up. Rose realized she would need to up her game a little and dress nicely enough to impress the judges and public as one of the figureheads of a winery. Most of her outfits were pants suits for the courtroom. She did manage to find a dark blue dress with a small white fleck pattern which she figured would look fine. She put the dress on along with some white heels, like Lea, but she decided to go plain and not accessorize. She made sure her hair looked nice, but she decided against makeup.

    "Hurry up Rose! We're going to be late." She heard Lea call out. Rose left her room and remembered she needed to bring the check to pay Ryan and his men. She went into her office and got the envelope with the check and turned to look at a picture of her mother and father. In the picture, they were each holding up a bottle of wine and smiling. She whispered to the picture, "Today is for you both. We'll show everyone how good your wine is."

Rose heard a slight cough behind her and turned to face Manuel.

"This is your day too. You and your sister. You two have worked so hard these last few months. I know your parents are very proud of you both."

"Thanks, Manuel. I still can't believe they are gone."

"Grief takes time to heal. We are all still in some shock, but we must go on. We must live. That is as it should be and I know it is what they would want."

"Are you and Isobel going today, Manuel? It would be nice to have you both there. You know we think of you like parents too."

"Ah, Rose. You are sweet, but I'm still not ready to be bumped and jostled by all the people who will be there. And aye Dios mio, can you imagine what they will be like after they have some wine and are starting to lose their balance? Ha, no thanks, but Isobel is going." Manuel said with a light chuckle.

"I understand. I'm glad you are getting better and we don't want to jeopardize that. Manuel, are you feeling well enough that I can hug you?"

Without saying a word, Manuel gave Rose a big smile and outstretched his arms to welcome her hug. Rose hugged him lightly as she was careful of his back. She held onto him, fantasizing he was her father. She only let go when Lea yelled again for her to hurry.

89

"Sorry, Manuel. I have to go."

"All my prayers are that today goes well for you Rose," he said to her back as she strode away to find Lea.

The girls jumped into Lea's Volkswagen and they made it just before the judging was to start. The parking lot had been packed, but luckily, they found a spot as Lea's car was so small. The sisters had to wade through hundreds of wine enthusiasts who had turned up for the judging. Although the winery that won the bid to host would make the most of food and drink concessions, the admission costs went straight to the competition committee to pay for expenses. Some of the competing wineries were allowed to pay the hosting winery extra for a six-foot table to sell their wine, but Chateau Baudin Winery just could not afford to this year and as Rose passed these tables, she hoped she might be able to next year.

Although Rose and Lea had grown up at their family's winery, they still knew very few faces in the crowd. They both had been mostly away for the last few years and the Temecula Wine Valley had exploded with new wineries, which meant new jobs and new faces. Working their way closer to the judging table, which had been set up on a short stage so people could better view the process, they found Isobel near the front. They all hugged each other for good luck and afterward Isobel also did a silent prayer followed by the Sign of the Cross. Just as the tension in the room was about to burst with the inevitable beginning of the judging, Rose felt a strong tap on her shoulder.

"Ouch! That hurt. What do you...Oh, it's you, Ryan. Hello."

"Hey, I thought you were going to look for me."

"Why bother? I knew you would find me since I have your check." Rose pulled the envelope with the check out of her handbag and handed it to Ryan with a smile.

"Great. Thanks. Sorry if I tapped you too hard."

Lea had heard their exchange and started laughing hard. Rose looked at her vexedly and asked, "And what is so damn funny?"

Between laughing, Lea blurted out, "It's about time someone tapped you hard!"

Rose turned a shade of red and wanted to hit her sister. She turned to Ryan quickly and stammered out, "I'm sorry. My sister is rather juvenile at times. I'm still waiting for her to grow up." Ryan looked appraisingly at Lea, now under control of her laughing, and said, "She looks pretty grown up to me." Rose was just about to say something profane to Ryan but was stopped by the announcement the judging would now commence.

Over the loudspeaker, a man's voice said, "Ladies and gentlemen, welcome to Chateau Tautou, our gracious host for this year's wine competition. Twenty-two of the local wineries have entered their best wines from last year's growth. These may be young wines, but they should have plenty of body and flavor. For our judgment today we have with us…" The man on the loudspeaker rattled off the bonafides for each of the hand-picked judges and then shared the list of the twenty-two wineries involved and which varietal each had chosen for the competition. Chateau Baudin, at number twenty-two, was mentioned last with their signature chardonnay. The man said the varietals would be judged separately for rank, but an ultimate winner would appear based on the usual hundred-point wine judging system. The hundred points would be spread over five main categories: the liquid is obviously wine and can be imbibed, color and appearance, aroma and bouquet, flavor and finish, and overall quality.

    Everyone watched the judging in rapt attention. Rose looked around her and was surprised at how seriously everyone took the event. Even Ryan was quiet and staring as each judge took a sip of wine, spit it out in a spittoon, and marked a number on their scorecard. Rose looked at Lea and saw she was actually biting her nails as she too was staring, transfixed by the judging. Rose felt some anxiety, but it was of a more practical nature. She hoped her investment in joining the competition would not go to waste. Five hundred dollars was not easy to come by, she thought. Even though she had made good money as a lawyer, she had a frugal streak in her which she felt she must have gotten from her father. Her father had been so careful with money and it was through his frugality the winery eventually afforded them a decent living. They were never rich, but they got by just fine. Her parents had enough money to at least partially help them with their education, but he still expected both girls to earn some scholarships and grants, which they both did. Rose listened closely as the final results came in just about an hour after the judging started.

Miller Creek Winery was announced as the top cabernet sauvignon with a total average of 90 points. Madame Tautou Winery was announced as the top chardonnay at 94 points and was also named the grand winner overall. All of the other wineries were announced by place and points. Chateau Baudin Winery chardonnay came in at 88 points. Rose felt devastated. Ryan tried to console her, "88 points is a good score. Your wine should sell well with a score like that."

"Don't patronize me. 88 points is a far cry from reaching even 90 points as far as wine is concerned. I never should have entered this competition. This has been a waste of time and money." said Rose as she turned to leave. Ryan caught her arm and spun her around to him.

"Rose, 88 points is not bad. Especially for your first attempt. You need to go easy on yourself. This year's yield may be better and you might beat these mega-wineries next year."

Rose pulled free of Ryan's grip and said, "What do you know? You're just a picker. You don't know shit about wine-making." and she stormed off. Ryan watched her walk away and Lea placed a hand on his arm and said, "Sorry Ryan. She's just upset. I think she had a lot riding on this. We both love drinking Dad's wine and believe in our winery. I think Rose just can't believe we are not the best. It's nothing personal."

"Sure. I know. She's just so wound up. She really needs to chill out a bit. I like your wine. With a little work, you guys might have something really special."

Lea smiled at Ryan and patted his arm then turned to leave to follow her sister. She quickly turned back and said, "Rose needs some good friends. I hope you will help her and be a friend." Lea left before hearing Ryan mumble, "Yeah…I would like that."

-

Two weeks had passed since the judging and Rose and Lea were both immersed in the fermentation process awaiting the finished wine to be placed into holding barrels and ultimately bottled. During this time, they did not discuss the competition. As the sisters were busy working, Isobel handled bottle and case sales to anyone who wandered by. Isobel noticed there was a small spike in sales and let the sisters know. Rose wished she had saved the five-hundred-dollar entry fee to create a tasting room in their garage, but decided to dip into her savings to make it a possibility anyway.

 She hired a crew to transform their two-car garage into a small tasting room and gift shop. She was surprised that with some drywall, paint, and a few other necessary things, they were able to quickly open a very rudimentary tasting room. Within the first few days of it being open, it was already attracting wine enthusiasts. Manuel ran the tasting room most of the day since he could sit a lot and the work was easy for him. On weekend evenings when they stayed open later, after Isobel's dinners, either Rose or Lea would run the tasting room. Ryan Alexander showed up one night when Rose happened to be on duty.

 "Hey Rose, how about a glass of your famous chardonnay?" said Ryan with a big smile as he entered the tasting room. Rose looked at him without emotion and said, "Oh, you mean our 88-point swill?"

 "Come on Rose, 88 points is not bad. I seriously like your chardonnay."

 "Why?" said Rose incredulously.

 Ryan had to think quickly, but his thoughts translated to words easily, "I saw how much your parents cared for their vines and for everything they did. I know your wine is made from the sweat, blood, and tears of true lovers of the grape. Last year was not a great year for many wineries and your parents faced a lot of hardships before they...well...I know a good wine takes love and determination and I think your parents had that. I admire their efforts and thinking about their sacrifices makes your wine taste like a winner to me."

"Okay, that was nice. You earned a complimentary glass of our signature chardonnay. It's only 88 points, but still nice." Rose poured the glass and left Ryan to see if other customers needed a refill. When Rose came back Ryan had finished half a glass.

"Seriously Rose, this is a great wine."

Rose started to soften and took his compliment, "Thanks, Ryan."

"Honestly Rose, this is great. I think it equals Chateau Tautou and maybe even surpasses it. Your grapes this year looked really good. Who knows, you might win the judging next year."

"Who says I'll enter the competition next year? It was expensive as hell. I think I would be better off spending the entry fee amount on upkeep or improvements."

"Maybe, but did you get an increase in sales after the judging?"

"Well…yeah…our…Isobel noticed we started selling more."

"But?"

"I thought it was just due to us finally opening up a tasting room."

"Wrong. That judging alerted wine enthusiasts to your precedence. A lot of people love an underdog story and you and your sister making a go of the winery after the deaths of your parents makes for an interesting story. People coming here know about your family and what has transpired over the last year."

Rose looked strangely at Ryan and said, "You're wrong. People coming here are just checking out anything local."

"No Rose. You're wrong. Ask your customers."

Rose looked at the three groups of people. A couple at the bar, two tables of friends...she decided to find out for herself. The couple at the bar told her easily that they had been at the judging and wanted to try their wine. The first table of friends told her that they heard about her parents passing and were thrilled she and her sister were continuing the family tradition and wanted to support their endeavor. The final table full of people mentioned they also had heard about their loss and the determination of the sisters to continue the family business. All of this was strange to Rose. These people did not know her parents or her or even Lea. How could they know what they felt? Yet here they were putting their money down on Baudin wine. Rose circled the room and made her way back to the bar where Ryan was.

"I think you might be right. These people all seem to know our story."

"See Rose, you guys have fans. Wine drinkers love a good story. I mean, it is kind of ironic too that your wine-making parents were killed by a drunk driver, but…"

"Get out! Now! I mean it!... Now!" yelled rose at Ryan while pointing to the exit.

"I'm sorry Rose, I meant no disrespect…"

"Out."

"Rose…"

"Out."

Ryan always had a problem with not using tact when he talked and he did not want to argue with Rose so he left. Rose waited until Ryan was gone and then she sobbed behind the bar, trying to hide it from her patrons. Ryan felt like an idiot and wondered why he always said the wrong thing. He meant no disrespect, but his thoughts often were vocalized before being strained through a filter of tact. Rose was angry at herself for thinking maybe this Ryan Alexander, who was also handsome, might be a good friend…or possibly more. No way would she allow her emotions to get the best of her anymore. After a few sobs thinking about her parents, she let her grief ease as she had guests to attend to. Her practical side usually won out over any romantic or sentimental side she had.

While Rose was on duty, Lea had the evening free to meet up with Colin. Now that the harvest was over and the wine was fermenting, she had a little free time and was eager to see where things would go with Colin. He had texted her non-stop over the last few weeks, sharing funny memes, stories from his daily life, hopes, dreams, and so on. She loved hearing from him as he was her main contact with what was going on with her university friends over the summer. Roxy had gone with her parents camping at Rosarito Beach in Baja for summer vacation and university resuming was still a week away. Lea had already decided she needed to take this year off from school to help her sister with the winery and Roxy had helped her pack up her dorm room before Roxy left for Europe. In her mind, it had been a long and exhausting summer and the main source of release from work and frivolity was Colin.

    Lea met Colin again in Old Town Temecula for food and drinks. They had a light dinner at a famous hamburger stand and then proceeded to bar hop. They talked, laughed, and kissed their way through several bars. Many of the bars had live bands playing, which made Lea happy as she enjoyed live music. At the third bar they went to there was a Social Distortion cover band playing. They were a little off-key, but Lea still thought they were fun, especially being on her third beer of the evening. She was relaxed and happy and out for a good time. Colin had been trying different cocktails all night. Lea remembered he started out with rum and coke and then switched to mojitos, then vodka martinis, and...she lost track of what he was drinking now. She looked at his hands and he looked like he now had a gin fizz. She was glad he was cutting loose a bit as he seemed so edgy at times. She smiled happily listening to the band play the Social Distortion version of *Ring of Fire* by Johnny Cash and she could not think of a better time than she had had in months. When the band ended, she clapped enthusiastically, but she heard some loud booing next to her and was shocked to see that Colin was berating the band.

"Boo! You suck! That was horrible. Learn how to play better or stick to working at McDonald's." Lea saw that he was also starting to seem unsteady on his feet and she sobered up and realized he was drunk. She knew she had to sober him up before he had to drive back to San Diego.

"Okay Colin, I think you need to stop drinking now. Let's go get some coffee." And she grabbed his arm to lead him out of the bar. Colin impulsively jerked away and raised a fist at her head as if he were about to punch her. Her eyes widened in horror, but he quickly stopped himself seeing it was Lea, and apologized profusely.

"I'm sorry babe. I thought you were someone trying to start a fight. I'm truly sorry baby." This drunken behavior went on as they left the bar. Lea stormed out with Colin in tow. Outside she yelled at him a little for being a jerk, but she caved in to all of his apologies and that wicked smile of his he flashed at her. That smile, those eyes...she melted every time thinking what a handsome man she had found and all the things which angered her about him just melted away. They made out while sitting on a planter in front of the bar before Colin suggested they go somewhere. Lea was just as hot for his affections as he was for hers and knew it would not be wise to take him to her home so they got a hotel room nearby. They both had to drive. Colin on his bike and Lea in her bug, but luckily the hotel was less than a mile away so they chanced not running into any police. They spent the night making love with a passion Lea had never felt before. When they were done and Colin had fallen asleep, she lay in bed dreaming about what their next steps might be. Should she move in with him? Would she marry him someday? Not now, of course, but sometime in the future, she thought. Eventually, she fell asleep with a smile on her face just being glad she had found her perfect man.

Chapter Eight

*"Most days I juggle everything quite well,
on the other days there's always red wine."*
- Rachael Bermingham

Lea tried to slip in at home without being detected, but the others were already enjoying an early breakfast. She walked into the kitchen a little sheepishly, still wearing her outfit from yesterday with messy hair and no make-up. She knew what they would think and she was right.

Rose was first, "Look what the cat dragged in." Followed quickly by Manuel, "I was worried when you did not come home last night." Which left it to Isobel to deflate the tension, "Okay everyone, finish eating before your food gets cold. Lea, sit down and I'll dish you up."

"Oh, please don't bother."

"Nonsense, hija. I have made plenty. Now sit down and eat." Lea gave her a quick smile and sat down. She realized she was actually hungry. As everyone resumed eating, Lea knew they would want some kind of an explanation so she gave it to them.

"I met up with Colin last night…"

"I don't care for that guy." was Rose's quick comment. Lea decided to avoid a confrontation with Rose and just go on with the explanation to get it out of the way.

"Like I was saying, I met up with Colin last night. We met in Old Town and ate a nice dinner, had some drinks, and watched some bands. We stayed out so late drinking that I thought it would be best to get a room and sleep it off before coming home."

Rose put down her cutlery and eyed Lea saying, "And did Colin share the room with you?"

"That is none of your business. I'm a grown woman and can do as I please."

"You're still a snot-nosed kid in my eyes. You've acted irresponsibly enough already and this guy makes you act even worse from what I've seen. He's trouble and you're going to get hurt."

"You have no idea what you're talking about Rose. Colin, that's his name as you know, treats me very nicely. He's a gentleman. So, he made a mistake in burning one of our barrels. Give it up Rose. I think you're just jealous because I have a man in my life and you don't. Maybe if you got that stick out of your ass that makes you so damn rigid, you would find a guy of your own."

Manuel quickly interjected, "Little One, calm down. We were just worried about you. These last few months have been tough for all of us and we just get a bit anxious. Please at least text us if you are staying out late, or not coming home, so we don't worry about you." Isobel added, "We just want to know you are safe. Your private life is your concern." Lea looked at Manuel and Isobel and relaxed a bit and said, "You're right. After what happened to Mom and Dad, I know we are a little worried about each other. I'll text in the future."

Rose crossed her arms and said, "Bet you won't. All you think about is yourself. You don't care if we are worried about you or not."

"Screw you!" said Lea as she bounded from the kitchen and away to her room. Isobel said, "That was not very nice to say. She has met someone new and is defensive. We must give her some space, but let her know we care."

Rose held her tongue for a few minutes as Manuel and Isobel cleared the table. Finally, she stood up to leave and mumbled, "Isobel, I may need to borrow one of your chanklas in the future." Isobel shook her head and said to her back, "Hitting your sister will only make things worse."

As Rose went out to check the stock in the tasting room, Ryan drove up in his truck.

"Hey, Rose. How are you?"

"What do you want?"

"Look Rose, I'm sorry. I didn't mean any disrespect last night. I thought the world of your parents and what they were trying to do here. I'm not your enemy. I just have a bad way of saying things sometimes. I guess I put my foot in my mouth at times."

"Why don't you put your foot in your mouth? That would be an improvement. Maybe it would keep

104

you from saying stupid things in the first place." She said as she unlocked the tasting room and stepped inside. Ryan tried to follow her inside, but Rose turned and looked at him angrily and said, "We're not open yet. You'll have to wait outside or come back later."

"Come on Rose. I said I was sorry."

"And you think that should just make everything alright?"

Ryan smiled at her and said, "Well, yeah. It works with most girls." Rose took a step closer to him, looked him in the eyes, and said, "Well, that's your mistake. I'm a woman, not a girl." and she slammed the tasting room door in his face." Rose went about preparing the tasting room as she heard Ryan's truck drive off. Inwardly, she wished he were smarter. He was tall, muscular, had brilliant blue eyes, and a great smile, but even with all that she thought it was too bad he was just another local yokel...a country boy bumpkin...or just an idiot...whatever. As a high-profile lawyer, she felt she needed friends who were at her intellectual level.

Lawyer...she almost forgot she was a lawyer as she was so immersed in the winery. She wondered if she was losing herself to her parents' dream and wondered again if she was giving up on her own dreams. Weirdly, she realized she had not been unhappy to be home and running the family winery. It was stressful with all the debts and demands and all, but it was kind of rewarding too. She loved the idea of working the land and making a product others enjoyed. It was only her sister who gave her so much grief. If only Lea could act more responsibly, especially with Manuel being unable to do any hard physical work. It was then she realized she may have to hire more help and this was not a welcome thought as they were financially stretched already. She knew she would also have to make a choice shortly between staying on at the winery for good or going back to her career in law. She finished stocking and readying the tasting room as Isobel came to take over and open up.

  Lea had gone to her room without eating and she was hungry and angry when she fell asleep. She slept most of the morning and woke up around noon. She heard her phone and saw there were several texts from Colin. He apologized again for his loutish behavior and told her how wonderful she is and how much he adores her. She smiled as she read his texts and forgot her anger toward Rose, but her stomach was starting to growl. Just as she was about to text him back to say she would call him later; he sent a text asking if she could go with him to the movies tonight. She remembered she was expected to run the tasting room tonight. She texted back: *Maybe. I'm getting lunch right now. I'll text you later* and she went downstairs to find something to eat.

  Isobel did not cook on Sunday mornings. Originally, it was because she and Manuel would go to morning Catholic mass, but lately, it was because

Manuel was still recovering so she stayed home to run the tasting room in the morning while also caring for Manuel. Lea had the kitchen to herself but was too hungry to cook a big meal so she just made a sandwich. She looked out of the patio window. The vineyard also looked so enticing to her. She easily remembered all the days she ran around the vines playing various games or just losing herself in thought. She took her sandwich and started walking down the vineyard. She was about halfway to the barn when she decided she might as well check on the fermentation tanks. Just as she walked into the barn, she almost ran into Rose as she was leaving it. Lea was in such a good mood thinking about Colin she wanted to say something before Rose did.

"Hey. I'm glad I found you. You were right. I should've texted you guys. I'm sorry. All good?"

"Yeah. Whatever." Rose started to walk past Lea.

"Hold up a minute. How's the fermentation going?" Lea knew she could distract her exacting sister by asking a technical question.

"Oh, everything's going fine. We had enough yeast for the yield of grapes we harvested so nothing will go to waste. Initial checks are good and if all goes well, we should have some great wine this year."

"That's great to hear. It was lucky you met that Ryan Alexander guy. His men did good work. He's kind of a hottie too."

"Yeah. Lucky."

"That's all you can say about him? He's a hunk."

"I guess. He's alright. A bit too thick-skulled for me though."

"Rose, he seems like a smart and friendly guy even without his good looks. Don't you think you judge men just a smidge too harshly?"

"It's none of your business how I judge men. What do you know about men anyway? All you date are boys."

"At least I have a 'boy' of my own. When was the last time you even had a date? You're always wearing your pantsuits as a lawyer or else you're in jeans and flannels. You don't get asked on dates because you dress like a man. Guys probably think you're a dyke."

Rose made fists with her hands and her face had turned red from the exchange, but she composed herself enough to walk away without saying a word in reply. Lea, now alone in the barn, realized she had screwed up. She was going to be nice, distract her sister, and then ask Rose to work her shift tonight so she could go out with Colin again. "Shit," she mumbled and wondered how she would be able to see Colin tonight now.

After leaving the barn, it was Rose's turn to storm off upstairs. She went to her office, slammed the door, and sat down, stretching out her arms on the desk, planting her forehead in between them on the desktop surface. She was angry, yet felt close to crying as well. She was frustrated that her sister was not a good business partner, but it was more than just that. Her sister hurt her in her femininity. She tried to keep it hidden within her, but the truth was that Rose, the fearless lawyer, had always lacked confidence in her looks and dress. The pantsuits were her attempts to look like other lawyers for added validity just as the jeans and flannels made her look like a ranch hand. She knew the name for it was Imposter Syndrome. It was the perfectionist in her. She always wanted to be the best at everything she tried and thought dressing the part would help and give her credibility with others.

    She would never allow herself to wallow in despair for long and soon sat up, shook off her blues, and started thinking practically again. Her thoughts drifted back to the need to hire some additional workers. The winery could not really afford to hire right now, she thought, but she also knew she had to take the risk that with additional help the winery could produce so much better and efficiently. Besides, having Manuel unable to do some of the heavy lifting around the place was starting to show. Lea was pushing herself to be as helpful as possible, but even with her hard work, there was still too much that needed to be taken care of.

    Things needed repairing and soon the yearly process of pruning, then bleeding, then tilling, then planting, and so on, would all need to get done. The problem was she did not know many people in the area anymore. She wondered how to best get the right kind of help she needed. Finding the right men, or women, for vineyard work could prove difficult. She finally thought of how easily Ryan Alexander had gotten a crew together to help with their harvest. She decided to swallow her pride and call him.

"Hello, Rose."

"How did you know…oh yeah" she remembered that cell phones listed who was calling. Before she could say anything more, Ryan quickly said, "Look, I'm sorry for what I said. I'm a hard worker, but not much of a talker I guess."

"Forget it. That's not why I'm calling. I wanted to thank you for getting those guys to help with the picking. I thought it over and realized we were really lucky to have your help with that. I was wondering if any of your men might be looking for year-round steady work?"

"Hmm…Maybe. How many guys do you need?"

"Well, realistically just one to start with. We would only be able to match whatever they have been making, but we could also feed them and provide makeshift quarters in our barn."

"A meal and a hard floor. Sounds really glamorous." Ryan said sarcastically.

Rose took a deep breath to control her rising anger before replying, "I can't do any better right now, but we would treat them with respect and work around their schedule as much as possible. Do you think you know anyone who might be interested?"

"I think I might know a guy or two. Would you want to meet them and interview them?" Rose had not thought of that, but quickly picked up on the idea.

"Yes. If you can have them come by tomorrow at noon, I will interview them in our tasting room. Will that work?"

"Yeah. That should work. I'm sure I could get a hard worker or two to swing by."

"Great. Thanks. Bye." and she hung up without awaiting another reply. She didn't know what it was about Ryan that got under her skin so much. He was always nice to her, but she seemed to get easily offended by what he said. She spent the rest of the afternoon tackling paperwork. It wasn't until it got dark that she decided to stop work. Her thoughts turned to her sister and she thought she should go into the tasting room and check on her. Maybe she could explain how she has Imposter Syndrome and Lea might understand her better and not attack her femininity.

As soon as she entered the tasting room, she saw Manuel behind the bar. She went right up to him and demanded, "Where is Lea? Why are you here when you should be resting?"

"Please, sit and calm down. I will tell you my Little One." Rose was infuriated Lea was not doing her duty, but she sat down ready to listen.

"You see, Lea is in love and wanted to see her Colin. She asked me if I would take her shift and since I wasn't doing anything anyways, I told her that was fine. Don't be angry. It was my choice."

"Don't be angry? This is so typical of her. Her flakiness. How can I not be angry when she is imposing on your goodwill?" Before Manuel could reply, she stormed off into the house and upstairs, again, but this time to her room. She was so overcome with refreshed anger toward Lea that she fell asleep with her clothes on thinking about her.

The next morning, she came downstairs and had breakfast with Isobel and Manuel as usual. She didn't want to ask where Lea was, but luckily Isobel told her, "Lea texted last night that she was staying over with Colin and she would be home later tonight." Rose acted like she didn't care, but the anger was still on her face, in plain sight. She went through the motions, carrying out her chores and various tasks until near noon when she went to the tasting room. Since it was Monday, the tasting room was closed to customers. She grabbed a baguette, butter, some knives, and small plates, and set them all in the middle of one of the tables. She selected a bottle of Baudin chardonnay and four glasses and also placed them on the table in anticipation of her interviews. She would get more glasses as needed, depending on the number of applicants. Noon came and no one had yet arrived. No bother, she thought to herself. They'll be along in due time.

At half past noon, just as she was starting to get anxious, she heard a car pull up and someone get out. In walked Ryan Alexander.

"Hello, Rose."

Rose looked stupefied, "What are you doing here? Where are your men?"

"They're here. I mean, I'm here."

"Wait a minute. You? You said you knew some guys…"

"I said I knew a hard worker and I told you I was a hard worker. I want the job. Meals, hard floors, all the glamor. I'll take it."

Rose laughed and said, "No. Not you. What about your men? No offense, but I'm sure Tautou can't run well without you."

"That's where you're wrong. I trained my men. They'll be fine without me. I trained them over several seasons. Instead of losing one of them, I can now take myself out of the picture and start a new adventure."

"No! Not you."

"Come on Rose. I've got great references and I've been in the valley for years. I've got wine in my blood. You've seen what I can do. Hiring me would be ideal to help shape your winery. Besides, I knew your parents and admired them, as I told you before. Come on. Give me a chance."

After a little more talk, Rose gave in and acquiesced to the idea of having Ryan around. He was strong and knew his way around a vineyard. Her practical side knew he would be a great addition and huge help around the place. He also seemed eager to help even though she had no idea why. Eventually, they poured some wine and made a toast to commemorate the occasion of Ryan being the first new hire under her management.

Lea spent two nights in Colin's arms since Manuel had covered her shift and she did not have one the next day. The first night they had gone to dinner and the movies and Colin had been wonderful. He opened doors for her, paid for the meal and tickets, and…overall… treated her well. At the evening's end, they decided once again to get a hotel room nearby. That first night they made love and slept in each other's arms. Lea felt so content and happy. The next day they spent wandering around Old Town Temecula, poking around in antique shops, and taking a long hike in the hills before finally having dinner early in the evening. Colin had been great all day to be with, but she felt he somehow seemed a little uneasy. At dinner, he ordered a whisky and coke and that seemed to draw him out of whatever funk he was feeling. He had two before they left the restaurant for their hotel.

Before they went to their room, Colin stopped at a liquor store and bought a bottle of rum and a two-liter of Coke. Lea told him she didn't feel like drinking anymore tonight as she had wine at dinner. Colin told her that was fine, but he wanted some for the room to help him unwind. Lea thought a nightcap would be okay, but she was starting not to appreciate how much he drank. She was also starting to think about him drinking and then driving places. After all, her parents had been killed by a drunk driver. But this was *her* Colin. She would help him. He would listen to her and not drink too much. He just wanted to relax a bit. That was fine, wasn't it?

Chapter Nine

"I cook with wine, sometimes I even add it to the food."
-W.C. Fields

    The next morning, Rose was awakened by the sound of a truck honking outside. As she lay in bed half-asleep, she hazily decided whoever it was had nothing to do with her and she should just go back to sleep. As she started to drift off back to sleep, the horn sounded again. This time she was fully awake and angry as she jumped out of bed and went to look out her window. Below, she saw Ryan Alexander standing by his truck, smiling up at her.

    "What the hell are you playing at? I was asleep."

    "Good morning, Rose. I came to bring my stuff over."

    "Right now? It's too early. I was trying to sleep in. I wasn't going to get up until 6:30." Just then, Rose's alarm clock went off and Ryan was quick to say, "There you go. Time to get up." Rose frowned and held her tongue as she went and turned off her alarm and put on a robe. She went downstairs, opened the front door, and walked out to the driveway. She went up to meet Ryan and said, "Like I asked, what the hell are you playing at?"

    "Rose, don't you remember? You hired me last night."

    "Yes. So what?"

"You said the job came with lodgings. I'm bringing my stuff over" he said as he waved his arm to indicate the back of his truck loaded with various items.

"I didn't think you would be over this early to move in."

"I'm working for you now. I need to get an early start on my work."

Rose knew he was right. Winery workers usually started work early to beat the afternoon heat. She grumbled a little but told him to follow her to the barn. When they got to the barn, she opened a door to a small, unused room. It had been sort of a makeshift broom closet, but it was the size of a large walk-in closet.

"Well, this is it. Not very glamorous and it will need some cleaning out, but it is free."

"Free is great here in Temecula. Looks fine to me."

"Great. Excuse me while I go and get dressed." Ryan went to grab his stuff to move in while Rose went back to her room to dress. She wondered if it was wise to have hired Ryan. He really seemed to get under her skin often and annoyed her. She took solace in the idea that at least she was his boss now and if he did not meet her expectations, she would let him go. By the time she had showered, dressed, and had a light breakfast, she went out and found Ryan was already repairing a stretch of broken trellis in the vineyard. At least he does seem to be a hard worker, she thought as she approached him and said, "Looks like you've already found some work to do."

"Yep. This probably got broken during the harvest. I'll be done fixing this soon. Do you have other things you'd like me to work on?"

"You remember our manager, Manuel. I'll send him out to you. He has a 'Honey Do' list of things which need to get done." Ryan flashed her another big smile as he got back to his repair work. Rose went back inside the house and found Manuel and told him about Ryan. Manuel agreed to keep him busy and he went out to find Ryan. Isobel had heard the exchange and asked Rose, "Did you hire this Ryan?"

"Yes. Sorry, I forgot to tell you and Manuel. He'll be living in the barn in the old broom closet room." Isobel smiled at hearing this news and for some reason unknown to herself, it seemed to annoy her.

"Why the big smile Isobel?"

"You got a good man there. Be nice to him."

"Isobel, he's here to work and he better pull his weight or he'll have to go. Sure, I agree he was a huge help at harvest, but we don't know anything about this guy."

"Hija, I know him. He did work for your parents on occasion. Sometimes even for free. Ryan, Manuel, and your father would work the vines together and sometimes he would stay around for dinner and drinks with your parents. He's a hard worker, but he's

118

also a good man. And very handsome too." Isobel spoke those final words as she turned to look at Rose with a smile and a mischievous twinkle in her eyes. Rose was getting annoyed at hearing about how handsome Ryan was. First, it was her sister and now Isobel. She had no interest in hooking up with a guy at this point in her life with so much work to do and her own career to figure out. She kept her annoyance in check and said, "Well, as I said, he needs to prove himself to me." and she walked out of the room. Isobel could not help smiling thinking Ryan would be good for Rose. She knew he would prove himself to her, and in time, maybe Rose would come to see his other qualities too.

-

    Lea had another great night with Colin. They made love several times as they stayed up most of the night. Colin had drunk a whole bottle of rum he mixed with soda during the course of the evening and it seemed to fuel his passion. Lea was used to getting up early, first because of school and now because of her work at the winery. She lay in bed, wide awake, listening to the sound of Colin's breathing and thinking she had found *The One* who might someday be her partner or husband. She lay in bed for almost an hour before she turned to look at Colin. His back was to her as he slept. She stared at his form just a little longer and then decided to gingerly wake him up so they could snuggle a bit before leaving the hotel for some breakfast.

    She finally moved closer to him in bed and was torn between running her fingers through his hair or just putting her arm around him and snuggling that way for a while. She decided to run her fingers through his hair. At first, he was fast asleep and did not seem to notice. As she played a little longer, he started swatting at her hand as if a fly was attacking him. She thought this was funny and giggled quietly as she started teasing his hair on purpose to wake him up. She just started again when he quickly rolled over and punched her in the eye.

    "Owwww! What the hell Colin! What the fuck was that for, you asshole!" she yelled out as she jumped out of bed and ran into the bathroom. Colin was still drowsy from sleep and hungover. It took him a minute to realize he had just punched Lea and she was now in the bathroom running water and crying. He got up and knocked on the bathroom door saying, "I'm sorry baby. Really, really sorry. I was totally asleep and I guess I thought I was being attacked or something. Are you okay? Please talk to me." He heard the water had stopped running and the door opened. He saw that Lea had a black eye. He had landed a good punch on her right eye. He winced when he saw it and said, "Oh man, I am so sorry baby."

    "You already said that. What the hell was that?"

"Like I said, I thought something, or someone, was attacking me. It was just a reflex response. I've never done anything like this before. I was just totally asleep. Please forgive me."

Lea was still a little shaky, but here she was in this hotel room with a guy she thought she was falling in love with, and had a quick choice to make. She either accepts his apology and they move on or she cuts and runs now. They had been seeing each other for just about two months. She knew she really had not known Colin long, or even knew much about his background or friends. She was weighing all these thoughts when Rose popped into her mind and she remembered how her sister was against her dating Colin. She made her decision. She walked out of the bathroom and said, "I accept your apology." Colin smiled and leaned in to kiss her, but she put out a hand on his chest to stop him and said, "Two conditions. One, this never happens again or I'm gone."

"Absolutely. I could never intentionally hurt you. You know that. I really like you. I'm filled with feelings for you I've never had before. I think I may even be falling in love." Lea was taken aback by this as they had never used the 'L' word before. She realized he hadn't actually said he loved her so this was a big step for him.

"What is your second condition? I'll do anything."

She looked into his eyes and said, "Second, you have to kiss my boo boo and make it better." He chuckled a little and leaned in and kissed her lightly on her swollen eye.

"Ow...it still hurts."

"Do you hurt anywhere else?"

"No. Just my eye. I'm going to look hideous."

"I promise I will still find you hot, black eye and all."

"Really?"

"Well, if nothing else hurts, I know how I can prove it to you." He leaned in to give her a light kiss on the lips, which turned into an even more passionate kiss, which turned into the couple returning to bed for another hour before they got their breakfast.

-

Around noon, Isobel made sandwiches and cucumber lemonade for everyone. She called out to Manuel and Ryan, who were working among the vines, to eat the lunch she had laid out on the patio table. She had also called out to Rose who was working in her office. The four of them sat down and shared how their day was going. Manuel was full of praise for Ryan and all he had already accomplished in one day. Ryan was modest and kept trying to place the praise back on Manuel and how good of a boss he was. Rose stayed quiet. She listened, but her mind was also on some bills she had to pay. The winery was making some money, but lately, she had been depleting a lot of funds from her personal savings and it was starting to worry her. Isobel was always so good-natured and listened to the men and laughed along with some of their little jokes about each other and how the other worked and so on. Rose had not even thought about Lea at all when she heard someone open and shut the front door. She thought she better see if it was Lea or a customer looking to buy wine.

Rose got up quickly and went toward the front of the house and caught a glimpse of Lea as she was halfway up the stairs heading to her bedroom. Rose called out, "Hey stranger. Finally came back home, huh? I'm glad to see you remember where it is." With her back to Rose, Lea froze on the stairs and replied, "Very funny Rose. I'm tired and just want to freshen up and take a nap. I'll see you later."

"Lea, this can't wait. I need to have a serious talk with you about flaking out on your tasting room shift. That was unfair to Manuel."

"Okay, I'm sorry. I won't do that again."

"That's right Lea. You won't. I told Manuel to never make a deal with you like that again. We all have to pull our parts equally."

"Is that all? I want to go to my room." Lea said with her back still toward Rose.

"No. There are more things we need to discuss."

"Can't it wait?"

"No Lea. As co-owner, I need your opinion on a few things. I hired a new worker and we need to plan some repairs and so on." Rose was starting to get annoyed at talking to Lea's back and added, "Turn around and come down. We really need to talk." She said with rising agitation in her voice.

"Rose, I really don't…"

"No more flaky excuses. You need to help me if we are going to keep the winery going. I need at least ten minutes of your time and then you can go relax. Come down here now."

Lea resented the command and turned angrily, faced Rose, and said between tears and anger, "Screw you, Rose! I'm not a little child you can boss around. I said I will see you later." Then Lea ran up the stairs and the sound of a door slamming shut was quickly heard. In that instance, before she had a chance to say anything, Rose had seen that Lea had a huge black eye. Rose immediately ran upstairs after her sister and tried to get into Lea's bedroom, but the door was locked. Rose started pounding on the door and loudly telling Lea to let her in. Lea repeated, "Go away." several times.

"Lea, what happened? Did you get into an accident or did Colin do that to you? Lea? Open up." Rose could hear Lea sobbing in her room, but would no longer respond to Rose's entreaties to open the door.

Rose finally gave up and went back downstairs and joined the others who were still finishing lunch. Isobel asked what the matter was.

With anger in her voice, Rose said, "I think Colin hit her, but she won't talk to me."

Everyone started asking questions at once, but Rose could only say, "All I know is that she has a black eye and is upstairs crying in her room and she won't speak to me."

-

It was not until dinner time when Lea finally made an appearance. Rose immediately began asking her again what happened and why she had a black eye and if it was Colin's doing. Lea had put cover-up make-up on so it was not as easy to see the blackened eye.

"Look, I don't want to talk about it. I feel like an idiot. I was on the back of Colin's bike and mis-stepped getting down from it and fell and hit my head on a curb. It's no big deal. I just feel stupid about it, okay? It was my fault and not Colin's."

Rose suspected Lea might be lying to everyone. Lea was flaky, but not known for lying so they all dropped discussing the matter. Lea quickly followed up with, "Rose, you wanted my opinion on some winery matters?" This quickly diverted Rose's thoughts to business matters and they discussed various projects and repairs as well as hiring Ryan Alexander.

"I think hiring Ryan was a great idea. He helped us a lot with the harvest."

"Yeah, Isobel vouches for him, but we just don't know much about him."

"Rose, you never trust anyone until they prove themselves to you. That's a terrible way to live."

"Lea, maybe you should not go around being so trusting of everyone."

The conversation went on like this for a bit before the sisters returned to the business matters at hand. Their talk ended when Lea received a phone call from Colin, excused herself, and went to her room to talk. Just then Ryan came in from the fields to get his dinner from Isobel.

"The amazing aroma of your cooking dragged me out of the fields." Ryan said playfully with a big smile for Isobel.

"Good. You need nourishment. Sit down and I'll dish you up." Isobel turned away to get Ryan some dinner.

Although Isobel told him to sit and eat, he said he would take his dinner to his room as he was tired. The truth was that he had seen the look on Rose's face and knew she needed some time to herself. Rose sat quietly as Isobel and Manuel cleared and cleaned up from dinner. Isobel had given Rose a glass of wine. Rose sat and sipped and thought of Colin. She liked men, but she was distrustful of them until she got to know them. She was pretty good at sizing people up and she thought Colin might be trouble eventually. She wondered some more if her sister had lied to her or not. She may never know for sure. She only thought of Ryan for a fleeting moment. He seemed okay. He was working hard already. Manuel had said he was an excellent worker and she valued his opinion so she left off thinking about him as she figured time would tell. Yes, time will tell when it comes to getting to know these new men in their lives.

Chapter Ten

"Wine is sunlight, held together by water."
- Galileo Galilei

    The last few days of September saw everyone pitching in with all aspects of maintaining the winery and preparing for winter to come. Ryan did most of the hard labor that was needed while Manuel supervised and planned. Manuel's back was healing well, but he often seemed short of breath. He often said it was his back muscles 'hurting while healing.' Rose and Lea often helped the men or took turns with Isobel running the tasting room. Thanks to the new room, Chateau Baudin Winery was gaining new customers looking to find that next special small batch wine. The tasting room was starting to bring in a steady amount of money, and Rose was finding optimism in planning on grounds expansions and product lines. Lea continued seeing Colin and no more had been said about the black eye. And Colin behaved as a doting gentleman toward Lea so she felt good about their relationship progressing forward. She knew mistakes happened and thought maybe Colin had some leftover post-traumatic stress from his tough childhood. She would be careful how she woke him from sleep in the future. All continued well as the calendar changed into October.

As Rose and Lea had been baptized Catholic but were descended from Jews, their family had always celebrated both sets of holidays. They even melded Hanukkah and Christmas into Chrismukkah and took care to decorate with the Star of David as well as with a Christmas tree and lights. The first week of October, the girls would celebrate Yom Kippur. This was a time for them to make amends and ask for forgiveness from God. Their prayers would coincide with a twenty-five-hour fast from food or drink along with refraining from work and a few other stipulations. This being the first year without their parents, both girls felt the need to pay special attention to the observance. They would not go to a synagogue, but they would make sure to follow the prohibitions; no eating or drinking, no bathing, no anointing their bodies with oil, no wearing leather shoes, and no sexual relations. The last prohibition had never been a problem, until now. Lea forgot the date of the observance and had scheduled a date with Colin. As sex always seemed to be the culmination of their dates, she was a little worried he might get upset with her, but she decided to shrug off these thoughts. He acted like a gentleman and would realize this was part of her religious beliefs and he would honor it.

    Things were going well in Rose's eyes. Everyone was hard at work. Things that had been put off, even when her parents were alive, were finally getting done. The cash flow was slowly increasing, which meant she did not have to dip into her personal savings as much. She still did not like that her sister was dating Colin, but she was glad she had hired Ryan.

He was certainly proving himself at being a great worker. She felt his only quirk was in being too talkative at times. It didn't matter whether she found him among the vines, in the barn, or at their patio or dining room table, he always wanted to talk. She found it kind of annoying that he was always trying to discuss such banal topics with her as the weather, things about his family or telling her what he was currently working on even though Manuel always kept her apprised of their work.

The worst was whenever he would ask her some random question about her likes or dislikes. Things like what she likes to eat. Does she ever wear jewelry, and if so, what kind does she like? Gold or silver? Things made of more natural materials like wood? She found his curiosity annoying and unnecessary. She only kept from chiding him as he was such a good worker and Manuel vouched for his efforts. His quirk of having such a talkative nature would just have to be tolerated as she realized it would not be beneficial to lose him. She also contented herself by thinking Ryan was just curious because he was new at Chateau Baudin Winery and would eventually stop asking so many questions.

The night of Yom Kippur, The Day of Atonement had arrived. Just before the sun went down, the sisters enjoyed one of Isobel's great meals and drank a lot of water. Once the sun was down, their fast began. This was the one time of year Rose actually allowed herself to rest. She had bought a new book and retired early to her room to observe Shabbat Shabbaton, an observance of solemn rest. She assumed Lea would do the same, but Lea was not like Rose and figured going out with Colin for an evening walk or a movie would be okay. Her family had never been too strict about Yom Kippur, especially as they were also Catholic, but she knew she could not eat, drink, or do anything strenuous, like work or sex. Seeing a movie was borderline on the list of prohibitions for this holiday. She had already explained all of this to Colin. He said he totally understood and they would go for a walk and a movie then call it a night. No problem.

    Lea did not want to hear any admonishments from Rose so she waited until Rose was well ensconced in her room before she quietly left the house and drove off to meet Colin. She arrived at the movie theater and found him waiting for her in the parking lot.

    "Hey there my sexy Jewess. Happy Yom Kippur." Colin said with that disarmingly winsome smile of his. It always seemed to make Lea melt a little inside, but she had to correct Colin on the things he said as they did not sit well with her.

    "Hello, Colin." She said, returning his greeting with her smile, but she continued, "I'm glad you think

I'm sexy, but please don't call me a Jewess. When I hear that I think of old wrinkled women in heavy shoes hiding their jewelry and saving bits of string for the future when a string, or whatever, may be hard to find."

"I'm sorry Babe. Okay...no Jewess. Got it. I can at least still call you sexy, right?"

Lea's smile deepened, exposing her dimples, "Of course." she said in reply, but again she had an addendum to make, "But, I think I should also tell you that you should never wish a Jew 'Happy Yom Kippur.' Yom Kippur is our holiest day of the year when we confess and atone for our sins. It is our most solemn day during which we repent of our sins and forgive those of others to achieve purification. It is a very serious holiday and not a frivolous one. It is not a 'happy' holiday, but a serious one which hopefully leads to personal happiness."

It was Colin's turn to smile bigger than before as he said, "Whatever Babe. You got it." And he started walking toward the ticket window. Lea was unsure if she liked his reply. It sounded too dismissive of her beliefs, but she reasoned he probably understood and she was being too overbearing about it all. She followed him as he bought tickets and they went in to enjoy a movie together. Inside, he was about to purchase popcorn and drinks for them, but remembered Lea had told him earlier she was fasting and he said he would go without snacks too in support

132

of her fast. She loved this and was happy that he was attentive throughout the film, holding her hand. She loved holding hands with him. His hands were calloused from riding his motorcycle and she loved how rough they felt. She thought about how she was lucky to have such a rugged, handsome man in her life.

After the movie, they went for their walk as planned at a nearby park. It was early October, but in California, it was still warm enough for an evening walk without jackets.

"Thank you for taking me to the movies Colin. And thanks, too, for understanding about my fasting today. I appreciate your support."

"Of course, Babe. You're my girl and I want to support you."

They walked a bit holding hands and either not talking for long stretches or making small talk about the weather. Lea wanted to burst, as the sexual tension between them was building. Since getting together, they never had a date that did not end in a night of wild, steamy sex. They sat down on a bench for a while holding hands and talking about trivialities when Colin finally asked, "Is it okay to kiss on Yom Kippur?" Lea thought it probably was not a good thing to do, but it wasn't actually sex. It was just showing affection, right? "I think that would be okay. We just can't go any further, okay?" Colin smiled and looked like a ravenous wolf for a second before he whispered "Okay." and leaned in to kiss Lea. They kissed passionately for a while, sitting on the park bench before Colin pulled away and also turned his head away from Lea.

"What's wrong Colin?"

"This is hard. I know we can't do more, but I really want to be with you."

"You know we can't have sex. Not today."

"I know. I get it, but I wish our date didn't have to end. I wish I could just hold you all night."

"I'm here. You can hold me as long as you like."

"I know. I just wish we could stay together all night and wake up together, watching the sunrise. Maybe get breakfast together. I have so much school stuff to work on, I'm not sure when I can see you again and I hate losing any opportunity to be with you."

"Well, there just isn't anything we can do today. I can't eat or have sex today."

Colin turned to meet her eyes and there was a hint of anger in them as he said, "You don't have to keep telling me that. I get it. I do. I just want to hold you all night long. Is that wrong?"

"No, my darling," she said as she reached out and stroked his hair, "I'm glad you want to hold me."

"There must be something we could do, but what?"

"No, I think tonight we just have to keep love in our hearts and wait until our next date. I promise I will make it up to you."

Colin was quiet for a moment before he said, "I have an idea. I know we can't have sex, but I can kiss you and hold you, right?"

"As long as you like, my darling boy."

"What if we get a room and just fall asleep holding each other? Then we can wake up watching the sunrise and get breakfast like I said." Lea's mental alarm was going off. She knew being in a hotel room with Colin always led to much more than holding each other, but he pleaded with her and promised to act like a gentleman. She believed in him and finally consented. She knew she had her car and if things started going too far, she would leave. She felt it would be nice to fall asleep in his arms and she was starting to get tired.

They went to their usual hotel, got a room, and went in. They took off their clothes, leaving their underwear on as they slipped into bed. True to his word, Colin held her and stroked her hair without demanding more. They were both a little too keyed up to sleep and Colin said he wanted to smoke a cigarette. They were in a non-smoking room, so he said he would go out for a moment and be right back. She did not like that he smoked, but she understood he felt the need for it and said "Okay, but hurry back." The moment Colin left, she was starting to get sleepy. She hoped he would come back quickly before she fell asleep.

She was awakened by the sound of Colin stumbling back into the room. She could smell the smoke wafting in with him and he was holding a bottle of something.

"Colin? Are you okay?"

"Yesh…I'mm fine. I just had a lil' ol' smoke and got thirsty. I tried not to drink for your sake, but hey…I'm not Jewish. So, I went to the liquor store next door and got a drink. My cigarettes made me thirsty." Lea could see he had a bottle of rum as Colin was taking liberal sips from it.

"Darling, you had your drink. Please come to bed now and hold me. I'm tired and want to fall asleep with you."

"Insh a min…minute." he slurred before chugging a quarter of the bottle.

"Colin, stop drinking. Come to bed."

"No…heh…okay. Here I come." Colin took his clothes off again, but this time he got completely naked before sliding under the covers. He put his arms around Lea and started kissing her passionately again like he did at the park. She let him for a little bit. She thought it would get him tired and he would fall asleep. She hated the taste of the cigarettes and rum on his breath, but she tolerated it for his sake. During their kissing, he started rubbing her breasts and she repeatedly stopped him by moving his hands away. She finally had enough and said, "It's time to sleep Colin. Please go to sleep." and she rolled on her side, away from him to stop the kissing and groping. He moved up alongside her and held her arms. He could feel his swollen member pressed up against her.

"Yeah. You're my girl."

"Yes, Colin. I'm your girl. Now go to sleep. I'm tired and we both want to get up early to see the sunrise."

"You're my girl," he repeated in a drunken slur before trying to take off her panties. She told him to stop and leave her alone, but he kept repeating, "You're *my* girl." Although Lea was strong, he had her pinned and managed to tear off her panties. She was about to scream, but he covered her mouth with one large hand as he used the other to hold her down.

-

Isobel and Manuel never cooked, even for themselves, during Yom Kippur in support of the family during their fast. They wouldn't work, but they still ate. During the family fast, they usually went out to eat breakfast at a cafe they liked in downtown Temecula. When Rose woke up, she figured she had the place to herself and decided to go for a little walk amongst the vines.

She loved being in the vineyard during the early morning hours as the dew was still on the leaves and the sun was just starting to come out to warm everything up as the birds chirped their 'good mornings' to each other. Although the grapes had been harvested, she loved thinking about the cycle of growing and that wine was really like bottled sunlight. Maybe that was why people loved drinking wine in the evenings or in wintertime, to remember the sunlight. Hard liquor might warm you up on a cold night, but drinking wine was truly the civilized way of enjoying life, she thought as she walked around the family winery.

Rose was lost in her reverie when she heard a voice behind her say, "I thought I heard someone out here." She turned and saw Ryan Alexander as he moved from out of the shadows of the barn doors and joined Rose among the vines.

"Good morning to Rose. Taking a walk or were you looking for me?"

"Good morning. Just walking. No work today."

"No work? That doesn't sound like you. You're always hard at work."

"I'm on holiday."

"Holiday?"

Rose was getting annoyed by Ryan's constant questions. She was his boss and co-owner of the winery. She didn't have to answer him, but she reasoned it might seem unusual to him so she gave in with an answer.

"My family is half-Catholic and half-Jewish. If you stay on with us, you will see that we celebrate both sets of holidays. During winter, we combine Christmas and Hanukkah into what we call

Chrismukkah. We decorate both ways too. My family has always tried to be inclusive rather than exclusive and we also honor Isobel and Manuel by participating on days like Dia de los Muertos, to honor their ancestors and so on."

"Don't worry, Rose. I plan on staying on."

She turned on him and said, "Is that all you got out of what I said?"

"Well, that and yabba yabba about holidays. I get it. I like to hoist a few for every holiday too no matter whose holiday it is. What holiday is it now?" She felt horrified at how Ryan had seemed to decimate her feelings for the holidays into just another excuse for a drink. He saw the rising anger in her expression and added, "I remember your parents were not churchgoers. I know they had their beliefs, but they were not strict."

She finally spurted out, "How dare you talk about them like that. You obviously did not know them well at all. Our family beliefs were...are important to us."

"Look Rose, I meant no disrespect. I had long conversations with your dad and he loved life more than religion. He really believed in living by the Golden Rule. You know, do unto others as you would have them do unto you and all that. He believed life was too short to get wrapped up in the trappings of religion, or politics for that matter. He loved the simple things. Loving his family, growing his grapes, and so on. That's how I remember him. I know he celebrated holidays, but he celebrated life even more."

She wanted to run off in anger or even yell at him, but she knew he was right. He did paint an accurate profile of her father. He had raised his family to honor the holidays, but they were never slaves to them. She turned away from Ryan and continued with her walk. She figured he might have sense enough to go back to work and leave her alone with her thoughts and newly raised anger, but no, he continued to follow her to her dismay.

"So, what holiday is it?"

"If you must know, it's Yom Kippur. A Jewish holiday."

"Oh yeah, that's the one where you don't eat or drink all day. Am I right?"

"Yes."

"I once brought some beer over to talk over something with your dad and he had to refuse. We talked while I drank. I always felt bad for him about that."

"You could've supported him by not drinking in front of him."

"Naw, the beer was ice cold and it was a hot day. I remember. Besides, he said it was fine."

"He was probably just being polite. Don't you have some work to do?"

"Not right now. I did everything Manuel told me needed doing and now I'm waiting for him to come back to see what else he has for me. I'm all yours until he gets back."

"Lucky me."

"Yeah?" he said as a big grin crossed his face.

"No. I was being sarcastic. I would prefer to be alone."

"Come on Rose. You're kidding me. No one likes to be alone."

"I do. I'm an independent woman and likely to become a spinster."

"No way. You're too pretty for that."

She turned to face him again with renewed anger, "What? Too pretty to be independent?"

"Naw, too pretty to remain a spinster."

"I'm far too smart to become trapped by some guy just because he likes the way I look."

"Sure. Not trapped by some guy, but many guys would want to be with a woman as pretty...and smart...as you."

"So, you do think I'm smart and not just a pretty face?"

"Well, of course. You just need the right guy to come along and show you what's what."

"Oh, so I need a man to show me the way?"

"Yeah, sort of. It takes two halves to make a team. The right guy could be just what you need to sort you out."

With mounting, anger Rose replied, "A man to show me...to sort me out. I guess I'm lucky to have you and Manuel, as males, here on the vineyard or poor little old me could never make a go of it or even make a decision." She wanted to say more, but she finally decided this time to storm off back toward the house. Ryan realized he pissed her off and said to her back, "I just meant you need a partner for help and support in life. We all do." She did not reply, but she thought to herself she had a partner. Her sister. Lea might be a flake at times, but they were blood and they would always try to work things out, to compromise. They did not need men for that.

Chapter Eleven

"Winter gives me something to wine about."
- Anonymous

As the morning wore on, Isobel and Manuel had returned from their cafe breakfast and Manuel had rejoined Ryan to check on fermentation and discuss the upcoming bottling and pruning of the vines once the weather changes. Isobel found Rose reading her book on the large living room couch.

"Good morning, Rose. How are you?"

"I'm fine, thanks."

"I know you are fasting, but what would you like me to fix for after sundown?"

"You know, tacos sound grand. Maybe chicken and carne asada?"

"Si, hija. I will gladly make tacos for you. Do you think Lea will be good with that?"

"I'm sure she will, but you can ask her if she wants something else or a special side or dessert or whatnot."

"Okay, but do you know where she is?"

"She should be in her room."

"No. Her car is gone. She left last night and has not been back yet."

"Really? She knew it was Yom Kippur. Where would she go?"

"Maybe to see Colin?"

"No…well, maybe, but I wouldn't think she would do anything to dishonor the holiday."

"I don't think so either, hija. Perhaps they are just relaxing together and he's supporting her during her fasting."

Just as Rose was starting to wonder just how wild Lea might be now that their parents were no longer around, she heard a car drive up. Isobel knew they might need some time alone to talk. She hoped Rose would not be too tough on Lea as she left the living room. The front door opened and a tired and disheveled-looking Lea walked in.

"And where have you been Lea?" pounced Rose.

"Rose, I am not in the mood to talk right now. I just want to go to my bed and sleep, okay?"

"I want to know where you've been. You look terrible. You know this is Yom Kippur. I hope you didn't forget, especially if you were with Colin Bannerman." Lea did not want to answer as she attempted to walk past Rose toward the staircase, but Rose stood up and grabbed Lea's hand, and spun her towards her.

"I want to know wher…" Rose stopped mid-sentence as she looked at Lea and saw she had been crying and there were finger-like bruises on her cheek.

"Oh Lea, what did Colin do this time?"

"Nothing. Just leave me alone." Lea ran upstairs and slammed her bedroom door. Isobel had heard the door slam and came back into the living room and asked if everything was alright or not. Rose told her what she saw and Isobel told her it may be best to let Lea tell them what happened when she is ready. She reminded Rose that Lea was home and safe for now and her story could come later. Rose did not like this, but she knew her sister was often dramatic and with a shrug accepted Isobel's advice.

It was hard for Rose not to be working so she decided to walk out to the barn to see what the men were doing. She found Manuel and Ryan unloading a shipment of empty wine bottles. These had been ordered for the upcoming bottling.

"How's it going out here?" she asked. Manuel was just about to answer, but Ryan quickly cut him off by saying, "Great. We are nearly done unloading."

"That's good. Isobel is making tacos tonight, but we won't eat until late, until after sundown." Both of the men said that was fine and that they looked forward to Isobel's tacos. After the last box was unloaded, Manuel said he was feeling a bit done in. His back was still healing. He said he would go and lay down for a bit and left the barn. Ryan saw that Rose somehow seemed pensive about something and decided to risk asking her even though he had already made her angry earlier this morning.

"Everything okay?"

"Huh? Yeah. Fine."

"That doesn't sound very committal. I'm sorry if I angered you this morning. I really am. I never meant to upset you. Sometimes things come out of my mouth that don't express exactly what I mean. I mean…" she cut him off with a dismissive wave of her hand and said, "No worries. I allowed myself to get too hot about nothing. You have your beliefs and I have mine. I'm not angry at you anymore."

"Well, I am sorry Rose, truly."

"Forget it."

"It seems something is eating at you. Care to talk about it? I can be a good listener even if I'm not such a good talker."

"It's nothing, really. I just worry about my sister. I think she may have done something wrong. It might not have been entirely her fault though."

"Boyfriend trouble?"

"Maybe. She showed up looking pretty messed up." Ryan remembered the black eye and asked if she had another one.

"No. No black eye, but she did have some light bruising on her cheek."

"Do you think this boyfriend might've slapped her?"

"I don't know. She's pretty tough though. If he did, she would probably have slugged him back, but somehow, she seemed pretty defeated when she came in just now." They talked just a little more, but with no more information to go on, they switched to discussing weather changes and when they should start pruning the vines before Rose caught herself and said, "This is sounding too much like work talk. I have to stop. No work for me today, remember? See you at dinner." And with that she left the barn, leaving Ryan to his own thoughts as he watched Rose retreat back to the house.

    The rest of the day passed quickly and soon it was sundown. The men had finished their work and were enjoying some cold beer in the kitchen as Isobel made tacos. Rose came in and said how she was ravenous and could not wait to eat.

    "Yom Kippur is always tough on me. I get so hungry, but I do feel good after fasting. Anyone call Lea for dinner?" They all said 'no' and Rose decided to go up and check on her. She tried Lea's door, but it was locked. She knocked lightly while speaking, "Lea, dinner is ready. Isobel made tacos for us. Come down and eat." Rose heard some light noises and Lea replied in a whisper, "No thanks. I'm not hungry. I'll get a late-night snack if I need one."

    "Come on Lea. You've been fasting for twenty-five hours. It's time to eat. You need your energy."

    "No thanks, Rose. Please go away and leave me alone."

    "Alright, you don't have to get bitchy about it." Rose went down and rejoined the others for dinner and told them Lea was not coming down.
-

    Over the next few weeks, things seemed to go on like normal. Rose and the others noticed that Lea seemed a bit detached and sullen. She was certainly not her normal happy, bouncy self. They just assumed she must have had a bad breakup with Colin since she did not go out on any more dates during this time. She did her share of the winery work and appeared for all her shifts at the tasting room. Rose felt maybe she was finally taking the winery seriously and did not want to spoil the hard work she was seeing in Lea and so she gave her sister space and did not ask about Colin.

They decorated the winery for Halloween. The sisters loved Halloween and went all-out putting up fake spider webs with giant spiders, skulls with glowing eyes, a few full skeletons placed strategically and holding empty wine glasses, and placing hay bales around for people to sit on. They held a special wine-tasting party. The first glass of any of their wines was free and this drew out a lot of adults, without trick-or-treating kids, looking for something to do.

As soon as Halloween was over, Manuel and Ryan started pruning the vines. When the vine is dormant, it is time to clear away the shoots from last year. This keeps the vines from growing out of control and also allows for a calculation of the production, or yield, of each vine. Also, as there is a limited amount of nutrients in the soil, pruning helps distribute those nutrients to a few main shoots rather than too many shoots. The men worked the vines for a few days, pruning and hauling the pruned wood to a wood pile near the patio.

November was a great time for bonfires and the pruned wood ensured they had plenty of fuel for these nighttime fires where all of the family and workers would gather, and share wine and stories.

As a little girl, this was one of Lea's favorite times of the year. She loved the talk and the laughter. This year, however, she was not as talkative or upbeat during the bonfires. She seemed withdrawn to all. Instead of openly trying to cheer her up, they were all just extra nice and attentive toward her. Like Rose, they all assumed she had a bad breakup with Colin. As one late night wore on and everyone had gone to bed except for the sisters, Rose finally broached the subject.

"You have not gone out with Colin lately. Everything okay?" Lea was quiet for a moment as she continued staring into the bonfire, but finally replied, "Yeah, we're okay."

"Look, I don't mean to pry, but you've seemed pretty down lately. Has he been treating you okay?"

"Yeah, we're just taking a break. He calls me. We are both just busy. He's focusing on school while I'm working here. We've just both been too busy to see each other." The truth was that Colin tried calling her all the time, but she was avoiding him. She would only answer texts from him. Colin would send long pleading texts to her almost daily trying to apologize for his drunken behavior and his need to see her. Her text replies were short and curt. She was really confused about her feelings for him. She was so enamored by him before he…

Rose felt she was holding something back, but she knew if she asked too much, Lea might erupt in anger. She knew she had to handle her sister carefully. Lea was not as steady with her emotions as Rose was.

"Rose?"

"Yes?"

"How are things going with the winery?"

Rose was pleased her sister was taking an interest in the family business and began rattling off all kinds of winery-related information. Lea knew it was easy to distract, or 'squirrel' as they called it, her sister by changing the subject to something close to Rose's interests. Lea nodded her head but really did not listen although she did get the idea they were surviving. After a while, Rose stopped talking and during the pregnant silence, Lea asked another 'squirrel' question.

"How about Ryan? How is he working out?"

"Oh, he's doing okay. Manuel says he's a good worker, but I find him annoying. He talks too much and he's always asking me questions when he should just be working." Without really thinking about it, Lea said, "Maybe he likes you."

"No way. He's just a hired hand. He's just a big lug."

"He's tall and handsome. Great muscles too. Besides, he likes to talk to you."

Rose remembered thinking he was handsome, but also wishing he was smarter. She did not think she could ever like a guy who was not her intellectual equal. She didn't care if he had degrees or not, she just wanted someone who she could talk to about books, philosophy, art, life, and so on. She explained this all to Lea as the bonfire was dying. Lea was only half listening, but inwardly she thought they might make a good match. Rose would need to loosen her pride first and Lea knew this might be next to impossible.

-

The week before Thanksgiving, Rose received a call from New York. It was from her law office. They reminded her how she was going to contact them after the harvest, but they had not heard from her. They told her the partners of the firm had voted to let her go. She was officially without a law job. This hit her hard, but also steeled her resolve to make the winery a sound venture. She was tough and knew she could always fall back on law work if the winery failed, but she would not let her parents' dream fail. Besides, she felt it was starting to be much more than just her parents' dream. It was a concern for all, Isobel and Manuel, as well as for Lea and herself. The days leading up to Thanksgiving were tough on the sisters as they both seemed a bit glum. She sometimes shared personal things with Manuel and when he found her wandering among the vines, he knew something was up with Rose. He asked her what was wrong and she told him.

"Ah, Rose, do not worry, Little One. Trials and tribulations pass us as we survive the years. Surviving and thriving are the main thing and you are doing that. You are helping all of us to do that. There was a journalist named Mignon McLaughlin who once said, 'Spring, summer, and fall fill us with hope; winter alone reminds us of the human condition.' You are feeling a bit down right now, but spring will renew your hopes."

"Is that another quote you got from my father's books?"

Manuel smiled and said, "Yes."

"I know you're right. Troubles pass. I know that. It's just tough."

"Sure, it is, but you did not lose your law degree. You can practice again if you need to."

"Yes. I just feel that the life I created for myself is dissolving and being replaced by a life that I am not sure if I wanted."

"Rose, I have seen how hard you have been working to keep the winery going. I think you might not have wanted this life, here at the winery, but I feel like maybe you need it. Being here with us. Being embraced by the memory of your parents. Trying to cooperate with your sister on a common goal. Maybe this is the life you need. At least right now."

They continued walking along the vines together silently as Rose digested what Manuel had said. She always felt Manuel was a simple man, but he always startled her with his insights and knowledge about life. Finally, she said, "Thanks, Manuel. You may be right. I just need to come to grips with it all. I really wish mom and dad were here, but I am so thankful you and Isobel are here." She thought about telling Manuel he was like a second father to her, but she held herself back from sharing her emotions.

"Wisdom comes with winters," Manuel said as they started walking toward the patio.

"Oscar Wilde?"

"Yes, Little One." They went inside the house together.

-

By Thanksgiving Day Rose and Lea both seemed to perk up a bit. Isobel had enlisted Lea to help her with the cooking and this seemed to brighten Lea's mood. She remembered spending many days assisting Isobel in the kitchen when she was small. Isobel was always so patient with her. Rose had been the tomboy, out hunting lizards, while Lea enjoyed cooking. Manuel set the table while Rose sat in the office looking over some last-minute business. Just before dinner, she decided to make a final check around the vineyard. She went out to the barn to check that everything was ready for bottling the previous year's harvest of red grapes. The last harvest for her father, she thought.

She hoped it would make a good cabernet wine. Her checks indicated it would be good. They had decided to bottle it after Thanksgiving as this would be the quietest time for the winery. As she was checking the barn, she heard what sounded like old country music playing from somewhere. She tracked the sound down to the room Ryan was sleeping in. She knocked on the door.

    "Come in."

Rose opened the door and found Ryan lying in a cot reading a book. Next to him was a portable record player which is where the music was coming from.

    "Is that Johnny Cash?"

    "That? No Rose. That's Hank Williams. Here, I'll turn it off." He reached over and stopped the record from playing.

    "Records, really? That's pretty old school."

    "Well, after my dad died, I just couldn't bear to part with his collection. It wasn't big, but he had some classic stuff. Rock stuff too."

    "Cool."

    "What can I do for you Rose?"

    "Nothing. I just heard the music and didn't realize you were here. Don't you have somewhere to go for Thanksgiving?"

    "Naw. I mean, I could go see my sister and her family, but her husband is kind of a blowhard. He makes a lot of money on the stock market and likes to act like a big shot. I prefer to visit her when just the two of us can spend some time together."

"But it's Thanksgiving. You should be with family."

"I'm good. I've got my dad's records and a good book to keep me company."

"What are you reading?"

"The Maltese Falcon by Dashiell Hammett. I've read it before, but it's such a great book it deserves another read." Rose knew about Dashiell Hammett from her father. She was surprised to find that Ryan read books. She had judged him to be a television watcher like most guys she knew. Besides her father and Manuel, she really didn't know any other grown men who still read books. Ryan was a lug, but at least he read. That was a point in his favor.

"Well, why don't you join us for dinner? We're going to eat soon and there is plenty of food."

"Really? That would be great. I wasn't planning on going anywhere today, but I think I could make it to the dining room." he cracked a smile as he said this. For some strange reason, Rose felt compelled to ask Ryan to read her a line from his book.

"Sure. 'He felt like somebody had taken the lid off life and let him see the works.'"

Rose nodded and said, "Dinner's at six. See you then."
-

Between Thanksgiving and Christmas, or Chrismukkah, they had finished all of the bottling of the last of the cabernet their parents, Alain and Claire, had harvested. From here on out, everything they would create would be from their own efforts.

Chapter Twelve

"In vino veritas - In wine there is truth."
 - Pliny the Elder

Christmas was quickly approaching as the cool breezes of a California winter were felt throughout the vineyard. The vines were dormant, awaiting spring when their sap would start flowing again. There was little to do over the next month or two until it started to warm up again and the vines bled sap from the pruning in preparation for new growth. The vines would signal when the cycle started again.

Colin had continued his pleas to Lea and she finally relented and allowed him to visit her during one of her tasting room shifts. She told him to come at the start of her shift. She knew Rose did not approve of him so she made him come while she was working so her sister would not see him. This would serve another purpose as well. This meant she would not be talked into going anywhere with him. He seemed so earnest to apologize to her and make it up to her, but she knew what he did was wrong. She felt degraded and horrified by it, but he promised he would stop drinking. He just needed her to be by his side as he quit. He often sent long texts saying how sorry he was and that he would never want to harm her in any way, and if it meant giving up alcohol, then so be it. He had to have her in his life. He often texted 'You're my girl.'

There was an inner part of Lea that knew Colin was not a nice guy, but there was another side of her thinking that felt maybe it was just the drinking. She believed people could be reformed, unlike her sister's beliefs that '*A leopard never changes its spots*' as she often said when discussing others. She really wanted to believe in Colin. He made a huge betrayal of her trust, especially on a holy day, but she reasoned they were in a relationship and he did not understand her faith. On the other hand, she should just cut and run from him. 'Uggh' she thought. She was conflicted and that was how she came to allow him to visit her. He drove up from San Diego State University on his motorcycle and parked just outside the tasting room. There were a few patrons already inside even though the room had just opened. He saw Lea behind the bar and went and sat at one of the barstools.

"Hey, Babe. Thanks for inviting me over. I've really missed you."

Lea looked at Colin with mixed feelings, but his infectious smile and those bright blue eyes just seemed to melt any negative feelings inside her. It was at that moment that she decided she was determined to reform him.

"Hello, Colin."

"Is that all I get? No hug? No kiss?"

"Let's just start with 'hello' for now. We still have things to discuss."

"Okay, Babe. Whatever you say. You're my girl."

"Let me go serve these people their wine and I'll be right back." She went and took a tray of wine flights to some patrons who sat at a table far from the bar. She came back to the bar and was glad it was early and so few people had arrived so she could talk freely with Colin.

"Colin, do you realize how bad you were to me? What you did amounted to date rape." Colin tried to cut in with apologies, but Lea cut him off and kept talking. "You really hurt me. Mentally. You are supposed to be my friend, my lover, and my protector. What you did to me...some girls would've had you arrested for. I'm only taking pity on you for two reasons. I believe you are going to make something out of yourself after earning your degrees and I don't want to ruin your life. That is one thing. The other is that you have promised me you will quit drinking. Are you sure you can do that?"

Colin responded profusely that he would stop drinking and that he would never hurt her again. He said he was thankful she was giving him another chance and he dedicated himself to not blowing it with her ever again. After all this, they made a little small talk as the tasting room filled up. Lea was starting to get too busy to talk. She told him they talked enough for tonight and asked him to go.

"Lea...Babe...when will I see you again?"

"We are going to throw a Chrismukkah party and I guess I'll invite you to that. Rose can't object to your visiting then as we open up our home to everyone. I'll text you the info later."

"May I at least have a kiss before I go?"

"Are you sure you will keep your promises to me?"

"Absolutely. Scout's honor."

"Were you ever a scout?"

"No, but I promise. Anything for my girl."

"Okay. We'll see." she leaned over the bar and planted a timid kiss on his lips. He was hoping it would be more passionate, but he knew he was in the proverbial dog-house right now and had to tread carefully with her.

Colin left the tasting room and went out and got on his motorcycle. He took out a cigarette and had a smoke while he sat on his bike. He thought about how he would work hard to deserve Lea. He really wanted to. With her help, he felt he would overcome his problems. He finished his cigarette and threw it down by his boot and snuffed it out. He looked around and saw no one in the parking lot. He took out a small flask from inside his leather jacket and took a quick sip before starting his bike and driving off. Lea would help him quit drinking he thought, but he didn't think she meant overnight. He would need to trail it off by drinking less each day.

-

For Chrismukkah, everyone had invited people over. This was the Baudin family's biggest holiday celebration of the year and the sisters wanted to make it as festive as possible. They had different varieties of their wine all around for people to drink as well as non-alcoholic choices. They had hired a 'taco guy' who set up on the back patio and served a steady stream of tacos with several meat choices to the guests. The firepit was in full blaze and the music was provided by a classical trio Rose had hired. Colorful lights had been strung all around the house along with both Christmas and Hanukkah decorations. Most of their guests knew about their background and accepted the idea of how the family celebrated years ago. New initiates to the festivities usually understand without asking, but every now and then someone would ask and the sisters would usually say something like, 'Our family was Jewish, but then baptized Catholic during World War II to escape the Nazis. We've just stayed both ever since so we celebrate both holidays at once. The taco guy at Christmas is because we're Californians by birth.'

The Chrismukkah celebration was in full swing. Isobel and Manuel had invited several friends and their families over. Lea had invited some of her friends from high school and university over. Rose invited a few close friends and some local law colleagues. Just like Thanksgiving, Ryan Alexander was also invited and told he could invite a few of his buddies too. Rose was happy to see he had invited the men over who had helped with the harvest. Some of them brought their girlfriends or wives. Everyone ate and drank and talked. Lea's friend Roxy arrived and Lea nearly knocked her down while hugging her.

"Oh my gosh, I'm so glad you could make it, Roxy. I've been dying to see you."

"This is my final year at San Diego State and my last courses have been brutal. I'm almost seeing the light at the end of the tunnel though. I wish you were still in the dorms so we could find time to hang out more."

"Oh, me too! I wish I didn't have to take this year off school, but I'm really trying to help my sister here. I'm hoping we can hire a manager and workers who can run the winery for us while I go back to school and my sister can go back to being a lawyer. I do miss being in the dorms and hanging out with everyone. Thanks again for helping me pack up my stuff before you left for Europe. I'm so glad you are here now." Lea helped Roxy to get some tacos and something to drink. Rose saw Ryan standing alone and decided now was a good time to approach him.

"Hey, Ryan. No date?"

"No Rose, but we are standing close to the arch with mistletoe if you would like a kiss from a hunk like me."

"My, somebody thinks very highly of himself. Too bad the arch is over there and we are over here, far from being under the mistletoe. Besides, it would break the decorum of the boss and the hired help dynamic."

Ryan looked a little peeved at this and said, "Okay Rose. Or should I say Mrs. Baudin now?"

"Come on Ryan...I'm just kidding around like you are. I'm sure you have many girls who would love to kiss you under the mistletoe."

They both remained quiet for a moment as they both looked over the celebrants. Ryan was thinking about what Rose had said, but wanted to tell her she was the only woman he was interested in, but he just could not bring himself to say it. She had reminded him that she was his boss and that complicated things with him. She also did not seem very interested in him as anything more than a worker. Rose's thoughts were not in agony over Ryan. She really believed he was just teasing her and that a guy like him would have no interest in a woman like her. She felt they were from two very different worlds and she needed to find a suitor who would be more like her. She had nothing against Ryan and he had some great qualities, but she held onto the idea that she needed an intellectual dynamo of a man who was also business savvy. She sometimes wondered if she was looking for a man like her father. They say women often fall in love and marry a man who reminds them of their father. This did not bother her as she loved her father very much and was proud, he had been so intellectual yet also

163

operated the winery. A guy like that was what she believed she needed. She finally spoke again to Ryan.

"Hey, I wanted to thank you again for all your help and for joining us here at the winery. Manuel always brags about how great of a worker you are and his words are gold with me. Really, thank you, Ryan. We are glad to have you here."

Ryan turned and faced Rose and said, "You said 'We,' but how about you Rose? Are you glad I'm here?"

"Of course…We, myself included, I'm glad you're here. I think my parents would've been glad to know you came to work for us too."

Ryan only cared whether or not Rose cared that he was with them at the winery, but he didn't press the point any further. The night was just starting and he hoped to engage her in a more intimate talk later if he could. He just needed to get his courage up first.

Lea and Roxy sat at a small bistro-size table for two, many of these were rented for the party and had been placed all around for guests. They talked about all things, school, guys, work, friends in common, guys, surfing, wine, the winery, guys, and so on. The night was starting to wear on when Lea mentioned Colin had not yet arrived. Roxy's expression changed from a quick frown back to a smile after hearing his name. Lea picked up on this and asked her if she ever ran into him around the school.

"Uh, not really. I see him at some of the parties, but never at school."

"Didn't you two have some art classes together?"

"Last year, but no class together this year." Lea felt she was holding something back. She had never shared with Roxy what had happened between her and Colin. She was partially ashamed but also felt it was no one's business. Lea had also been very open about everything, with everyone, except about her love life. She was never a kiss-and-tell type.

"Roxy, do you know something about Colin I should know? We've been a little rocky in our relationship lately, but I am still seeing him and trying to be supportive of him. I feel like there is something you are not telling me."

"Well, if you're still seeing him then why did you ask me if I see him around school? Didn't he tell you he was no longer attending classes?"

"Uh, no. He never said anything to me."

"Oh, well...his grades were bad last year and they put him on academic probation. During the first quarter this year, he showed no improvement so they kicked him out. He wasn't going to his classes often anyway and when he did go, he was often drunk." Roxy was very matter-of-fact in stating this. Lea was shocked and needed to process all of this. She was also trying to keep her anger in check. She knew Colin had a drinking problem, but she reminded herself she was going to help him. As if on cue, Colin arrived and joined Lea and Roxy. Roxy was done talking about the matter as it did not pertain to her and had lost interest. Lea decided not to bring it up at the moment and the three sat, ate tacos, and talked.

It was finally time for family and friends to gather around the large Christmukkah tree in the living room. Everyone had either a glass of wine or some sparkling apple juice for a toast. Rose raised her glass and said, "I'm not much on making speeches, except in the courtroom, but I want to thank each and every one of you for helping us celebrate tonight. We are not only celebrating the holidays, but we are also celebrating that Chateau Baudin Winery is still here. We are still surviving and we know our parents, Alain and Claire, would have been proud to see all we've done to keep the family dream alive. Merry Christmas and Happy Hanukkah to all. Mazel tov!" As she took a sip, everyone murmured 'Mazel tov' and lifted their glasses at her, and also joined her in a sip. Lea had made sure Colin was supplied with sparkling apple juice as she stood by his side for the toast. There came a slight cough from the crowd as Manuel went and stood next to Rose and asked for everyone's attention.

"Loved Ones, you are all so important to us. I call you all our Loved Ones because it does not matter to us whether you are a friend or family, you are our Loved Ones and also a part of our hearts. My wife, Isobel, and I have been a part of Chateau Baudin Winery for almost thirty years. We first came from Mexico as fruit pickers…migrant farm workers. We were lucky because we met Alain and Claire Baudin during our first summer here. They immediately took us to their heart and into their home. They made sure my wife and I had everything we needed and in turn, we always worked hard for them. We loved them and they loved us. This is what makes Chateau Baudin Winery so special. It is this love. This never changed as they had two wonderful girls, Rose and Lea. My wife and I watched them grow into the fine young women they are now and we are so proud of them. They keep the Baudin spirit, the Baudin love, alive for us all. Although Isobel and I were not able to have children of our own, we have never regretted it as Rose and Lea have always been daughters to us. May the love always flow from the Chateau Baudin Winery just as much as the wine to come. May God grant Alain and Claire eternal peace. Salud!" Manuel lifted his glass in salute to all and took a hearty sip. Everyone joined him by doing likewise and responding back with 'Salud.'

  Lea quickly went and stood next to Rose while Isobel went and held her husband's hand. Lea said, "Okay before we all start crying, let's open some gifts." Gifts were passed out to every guest. Each person present received a gift-wrapped bottle of one of their wines. The family also took this opportunity to exchange gifts. Ryan went up to Rose and handed her a wrapped box while saying "Merry Chrismukkah to you, Rose." Rose opened the attached card first, which read: My fondest wishes for your happiness now and always. Merry Christmas and Happy Hanukkah, Love Ryan. She thought it was a bit strange for him to write 'Love,' but she just figured it was the holidays and people liked to be less formal and more overt in their feelings. She opened the box and found inside a beautifully stained charcuterie board and it was laser etched 'Chateau Baudin Winery' with their logo.

"This is beautiful Ryan. Thank you so much. What a thoughtful gift."

"There's more on the back."

Rose flipped over the board and in smaller text, it read: To Rose, who sways and dances with the breeze. Love, Ryan. She was a little annoyed to see the word 'love' again. Ryan quickly interjected, "That part about swaying and dancing with the breeze comes from a poem I read somewhere once. It was saying how the writer thought the most beautiful flowers grew in places that were clear and lush, but actually, the prettiest flowers grow in adverse conditions like rocky areas, where they force their way up and enjoy being free. Somehow the poem reminded me of you and your struggle to keep the winery going."

"Wow. That was really nice and thoughtful of you. Thanks again, Ryan." She was impressed to learn he read poems. She figured he must read only westerns or detective novels or something like that. Although she felt a little uncomfortable with his overly familiar nature with her, she was impressed to find he had some hidden depths.

After the presents had been opened, there was time for desserts and games. Some of the guests left after the gifts, but many stayed late to play games and enjoy one of the many desserts either Isobel had made or one of the countless ones others had brought over. It was well after midnight before guests really started disbursing. Even Roxy had made her goodbyes as she had a long way to drive back to San Diego. Ryan helped Manuel to clear up plates while Isobel tried her hardest to wrap up food and make guests take some home, begging them as there was just too much. She especially made sure desserts were taken away as she knew Manuel would be into them if they sat around.

Rose went out to help Manuel and Ryan after saying goodbye to some of the last guests and found Manuel taking in the last of the dishes while Ryan swept up. She sat down at one of the little bistro tables and let out a sigh as she took in the crisp winter sky. She could see quite a few stars out as there were not many lights around them and the sky was clear. She sat there, staring at the stars and remembering a simpler time when her father would point them out and name them for her. She did not notice Ryan's approach until he sat down at her table. They both sat in silence looking at the stars for a few minutes. Finally, it was Rose who spoke first.

"When I was little, my father would sit out here with me on a night like this. He would first make hot cocoa, then invite me out to sit with him. We would sit out here, drinking hot cocoa and he would tell me stories from mythology and how they related to the stars. He knew the names of the stars and would point them out to me. Those were beautiful times."

"I'm sure you miss him very much."

She nodded, "Yes, I do."

"Rose, can I ask you a question?"

"Sure, but hopefully not about the stars. My memory is a bit rusty now."

"Just about one star…you. You know, I've been working with you now for almost half a year and I was wondering…Did you really like the charcuterie board?" He just could not get his nerve up. He never had this problem with women in his past, but around Rose, he just wasn't himself. She gave him a funny look and smiled.

"Of course, I liked the board, Silly. That was very thoughtful of you."

"Uh, good, I'm glad. Listen, some of my friends and I are going into Old Town for New Year's Eve. The country bar is having a good band and line dancing, drink specials, and the works. Care to come out with us?"

"I don't know. I like country music, but I usually have too much to do around here."

"Come on, Rose. You have to take a break sometime. You can't stay tied to work every day. Even a field donkey needs to rest once in a while. You'll work yourself sick."

"Oh, so now I'm just a field donkey in your eyes?"

"No Rose…uhh…I just meant…"

"Stop. I know what you meant. I work hard and I should take a break."

He smiled at her, relieved she understood his meaning. She was a little miffed as she felt what she did was none of his business, but she realized he was just trying to be nice and meant well.

"Maybe. We'll see."

"Come on. There's nothing to do on New Year's Eve. Come out with us. You can drive in with me. I'll buy the first round even." His smile and enthusiasm wore her down.

"Okay. One night. I'll go." She reasoned one night out wouldn't hurt things, and she might have some fun.

Meanwhile, Lea was walking Colin out to his motorcycle.

"Thanks for inviting me tonight, Lea. I had a great time being with you. And no alcohol too. As promised."

"Yes, Colin. Thanks for sticking to your word. I'm glad you came, but there is something I wanted to ask you all night."

"Sure Babe. What is it?"

"How's school going?"

He chuckled and said, "Is that all? School is fine. I'm not doing great, but okay. Getting by. Why?"

"Roxy said she hadn't seen you around school. She thought maybe you had quit."

"Babe, what does she know? I rarely run into her at school as we no longer have classes together. I'm going. Everything is fine."

"I hope so. You always told me you planned to become an architect and make something of yourself. I hope you don't give up on your dreams."

"I know my Dearest. I'm trying my best. Believe me. Roxy has no idea what she's talking about. Wasn't she the one you told me would always get the most stoned and forget what her name was at frat parties?"

He had a point, she thought. Maybe Roxy didn't know and just assumed he was kicked out because she hadn't seen him around.

"Okay, Colin. Be careful and drive safely."

He leaned over on his bike and gave her a nice kiss. She was still not allowing him to kiss her too passionately, but she was more passionate than on their last visit.

"And don't forget Babe, we have a date for New Year's Eve. See you then my Dearest."

He drove off leaving Lea thinking about him. Maybe Roxy was wrong. It did seem a lot of people were somehow against him. He was really coming around though and keeping his promise not to drink and he seemed friendlier somehow. She really felt everything was okay now and with her continued support he would keep improving. He just needed someone good like her in his life. Colin thought so too, that he just needed to have her in his life, as he pulled into the parking lot of a downtown bar in time for last call.

Chapter Thirteen

"There must be always wine and fellowship or we are truly lost." – Ann Fairbairn

In the days between Christmas and New Year's Eve, there was not much work that had to be done. Rose was glad to see Manuel and Isobel taking time to go on walks together and just having the time to enjoy being around each other. Manuel's back had healed well and he seemed almost completely back to normal except for a slight intermittent cough. Everyone was happy to see him recuperating so well.

Rose and Lea had an argument the day after the Chrismukkah party. Rose questioned her sister about why she invited Colin and if they were still dating. Lea defended him and her choice to see him. She had never told Rose, or anyone else, about what happened on Yom Kippur and decided she never would. Colin was not drinking and he was treating her well. Even though he had hurt her, he had apologized, made promises he was keeping, and he looked at her with his big brown eyes and she would just melt. To her, he was like a movie star coming to life. She had seen the movie version of The Outsiders, based on the book by S.E. Hinton about young street hooligans set in the 1960s, and thought Colin was like those young men. He was a rebel, but he had a big heart and just needed a break in life. Subconsciously, she was determined to be his savior. She believed wholeheartedly in her rebel and wanted him to 'stay gold' always.

Ryan was starting to get on Rose's nerves. Whenever he would catch her walking around the winery, he would remind her of their upcoming New Year's Eve plans. She felt it was getting to be too much. She came in from one of her walks in a huff and threw herself down on the living room couch and counted to ten silently. Isobel happened to walk through the living room on the way to the kitchen and saw that Rose was laying with her eyes tightly shut and the muscles were strained on her jawline as if she were biting down hard on something. Instead of stopping, Isobel continued into the kitchen and returned with an opened bottle of wine and two glasses. She put them down and poured wine into the glasses.

"Hija, time to sit up." She said as she held a glass toward Rose.

"Isobel, I just need some time alone."

"No dear. The men are out so this is our time. Lea is tending the tasting room so it's just us two right now. You and I have not had a nice girl chat in a while. Here." Rose knew she could not refuse the strong-willed Isobel. Isobel was the kind of woman who could endure a lot, but when she has reached her limit or has decided on something, she is mulishly stubborn and just won't budge. Rose knew it would be best to just do as she said so she sat up and took the wine.

"Thank You."

"No problem. Some writer once said 'There must be always wine and fellowship or we are truly lost.' I guess we are quite a couple. I'm even using quotes like Manuel now. You know, I am always here for you whenever you need to talk."

"But I really don't want to talk right now."

They both took a sip of their wine. Isobel was watching Rose's face, but Rose was purposefully avoiding eye contact by looking elsewhere.

"What did Lea do now?" asked Isobel. Rose finally made eye contact with Isobel and said, "What makes you think Lea did anything?" Isobel giggled a little and said, "Because she is the only person who ever seems to get you this angry looking. All your life, I have never seen friends or anyone else make you as angry as you get with your sister. You know, they say we get angriest at those we love. Something about them not living up to our expectations, but we're stuck loving them anyway. Kind of a curse, I guess."

"Well, this time you're wrong. I'm a little upset at Lea, but mainly at Ryan." Upon hearing Ryan's name spoken by Rose, there was a quick twinkle in Isobel's eye, but she knew best to keep her thoughts about Ryan to herself. Rose needed to decide for herself about him.

"Oh? So, Lea did do something then?"

"Not really. Yes. No. Well, she invited Colin to our party and I just can't stand the sight of him. Lea has never said anything, but I haven't forgotten her coming home with a black eye a while back and then two months back it seemed he really hurt her again. She won't share anything, but I think he's hurting her somehow and that he's just bad news. I'm just worried about what he might do to her eventually. I don't trust him."

"I understand my dear, but that is not your decision. I worry about Lea seeing him too, but we should not get in their way. If we try to stop her from seeing him, you know it would just force her even more into his arms. She's got a rebellious nature, even if it hurts her."

"You're right, I know. It just sucks. I want to help her. I want her to care about herself and quit being flaky too. When she pulls stuff, like she did that time changing shifts with Manuel, I feel she is taking advantage of others to satisfy herself. Being selfish at the cost of others. We are all working so hard to keep the winery going and I just feel like she doesn't take any of this seriously enough."

"She is still just a young woman, Rose. You are a few years older and much wiser. You were born practical and also a wise soul. Some are and some are not. She is a bit wild and reckless right now, but she is a Baudin, like you, and she will find her way and settle down eventually."

"Hmph. I hope it happens before she gets herself killed."

"Rose, you can't talk like that. You must always wish the best for her and strive to impart your wisdom and advice in ways she will listen to. Be smart and use some psychology with her. When you want to give her advice, make her feel as if she had the idea and not you. *Work smarter and not harder* as I always hear you say."

"Yeah. Do you always have to be right Isobel?" Isobel laughed a little and said, "I am much older than you and I have the wisdom of my years. Besides, how do you think I ever get Manuel to get things done from my 'Honey Do' list?" They both laughed at this before Isobel asked, "And what about Ryan? What did he do?" The smile on Rose's face became a frown again as she replied, "Oh god, he's just the biggest jerk. Ever since I hired him, he's been bugging me. Every time he sees me, he makes it an excuse to ask me dumb questions and repeat himself over and over again. I thought maybe it would shut him up if I agreed to hang out one night with him and his buddies, but now he won't stop badgering me about it. It's just a constant barrage of chatter from that guy. Manuel always sticks up for him and tells me how great of a worker he is, but sometimes I daydream of firing him."

"Come on, you wouldn't really want to fire him, would you?"

"I guess not. Not really. I just wish he would not bug me so much. It's just frustrating." Isobel was about to ask her why she bothered to take so many walks among the wines or out to the barn if she wanted to avoid Ryan, but decided against this. She knew when a guy acted like Ryan was acting, it was because he was interested in the girl he was trying to talk to. Isobel was trying to figure out how to respond when Manuel walked in from outside and immediately asked Isobel if she would drive him over to the hardware store for a few things. Ever since Manuel had hurt his back, Isobel had taken to driving him places so he would not have to strain his back. She didn't mind acting as his personal chauffeur as she enjoyed being with him. She told her husband she would be right out and he went back outside toward the driveway. Isobel stood up and told Rose, "Men can be difficult or seem strange, but they are all like little kids at heart. Ryan is a good man and a handsome one too. Perhaps you can also work smarter with him and get him to act as you would like him to. I have to go, my dear." Isobel went out to join her husband leaving Rose alone with her thoughts.

-

The days went by quickly and it was New Year's Eve before anyone was really ready for it. Isobel and Manuel knew the girls and Ryan were all going out to join the holiday revelry and they would have the place to themselves. Rose told them to close the tasting room early and enjoy their evening together. Around noon, Lea started preening and preparing herself to meet Colin. She showered and then painted her toenails as well as her fingernails. She crimped her hair and plucked her eyebrows. Later she would put on her best party dress and some matching jewelry. The last touch would be her make-up before she went out. Rose had spent the morning and early afternoon doing some work among the vines and had come inside around two in the afternoon and sat in the kitchen and had a cold beer to relax. She was wearing worn-out jeans and a flannel shirt which now had dirt from the vineyard all over it. She was dirty, but happy she had gotten some work done without being bothered by Ryan. Isobel happened by and told Rose how her sister had already spent a couple of hours getting ready for tonight and asked Rose why she was not doing the same.

"Oh, come on, Isobel. I'm just going to a cowboy bar with Ryan." As she was holding her beer with her right hand, she made a sweeping motion over her seated body with her left hand saying, "I could just go like this and fit right in with all the other field hands and vineyard workers."

Isobel frowned at her and put her hands on her hips and said, "Rose, you are not a man and you should let others see that you can doll up with the best of them. You might even find a man, cowboy or not, who is interested in you. Maybe even someone like Ryan."

It was Rose's turn to frown as she replied, "Ryan? Yucch. Besides, I'm not looking for a guy. I'm an independent woman. I worked hard to earn my law degree and now I am working hard to run the winery. I don't need a man."

The frown dropped from Isobel's face as she pulled out a chair and sat opposite Rose. In a warm, but serious tone, Isobel said, "Hija, I know you're tough. You don't have to let a man take that from you. A good man...the right man, can add to your life in many rewarding ways. I never told you this, but I was determined to come to the United States with or without Manuel. I almost left him in Mexico and was about to come without him. Luckily for me, he knew he was the right man for me and came with me and has been my greatest friend, lover, and supporter. I almost left him behind. When I look back, I realize how he has been the best thing, the best person, in my life. He was the right man for me and he has proved it many times over the decades. We both have our regrets, like not being able to have kids of our own, but we are very happy with the life we have carved out for ourselves and you and Lea have been like our kids. I guess I'm just trying to tell you not to miss your chance at finding a great partner like I almost did. You need to pick carefully and let a man prove himself to you, but once he does, don't let him go. Maybe you will meet a great guy tonight."

"Okay, you wore me down. I still say I am not looking for a guy to be in my life, but I will 'doll-up' a bit to fit in with the New Year's Eve fun, okay?"

Isobel smiled warmly and left Rose to finish her beer in silence. Rose decided she would dress up, but she was positive a guy was the last thing, the last kind of trouble, she needed in her life right now.

Around six o'clock both of the sisters were ready to head out. Rose dressed in a tight pair of new jeans with a big belt buckle, her best pair of cowboy boots, and a cowgirl button-up fringe shirt with embroidery. She put on a little eyeliner and curled her long, straight hair a little. She took her best matching cowboy hat, but would leave it hanging back from the chin strap instead of putting it on.

Lea had on a rockabilly-type retro dress that was white with red fringe and embroidered cherries on it. She wore matching red heels and even had a little red bag that also matched the outfit. The sisters said little to each other, but they did acknowledge each other enough to say how cute the other one looked. Lea was really impressed that her older sister was finally dressing up a little and getting in the holiday spirit. She was careful not to overdo her compliments to Rose as sometimes they had the opposite effect. In the past, she remembered making a big deal on how good Rose's make-up looked, which made Rose feel she must have too much on and took it all off. Lea knew her sister could be tricky to deal with. She decided she just wanted them both to have a great night out so she was very judicious with her words to her sister.

Originally, Colin was going to pick up Lea on his motorcycle, but she decided to take her own car instead as she didn't want her hair and skirt to get blown all out of whack. Besides, even wintertime in California is chilly and her car's heater worked well so she felt it was best to drive herself to Colin. They had decided to start their night at a little bar they both liked in Old Town Temecula where they played hard rock and had a great barbecue. In the back of her mind, she was a little apprehensive about going to bars with Colin as he was not drinking and she was afraid the temptation might be too strong. He convinced her that each bar they would stop at would have free sodas all night, great finger food, and good live bands to ring in the New Year. She knew he was a big fan of live music so she gave in, but she still held a nagging worry about the temptation of being at bars. She reminded herself of the promises he had made to her and she consoled herself with those as she drove off to meet him.

Rose watched Lea drive off and even gave her a friendly wave as she left. Rose was about to walk to her car when she saw Ryan's truck approaching and remembered he said he would drive them to the country bar. She didn't like not being in control of things like driving, but she decided it was best to acquiesce as he had said he would drive them and she had accepted. This is what annoyed her about Ryan. He seemed to have a way of making her flustered. Something about him drove her to give in when she normally would not. She hoped he would not be too annoying tonight and was glad that many of his friends would be around in case she got too annoyed talking to him. Ryan drove his truck into the driveway while rolling down his window. He looked at Rose up and down and let out a slight whistle before saying, "You look great Rose. Really beautiful."

Although she did not appreciate his informal attention, after all, he was her worker, she smiled and said, "Thanks. I clean up pretty well, I guess."

"I'll say you do." Ryan sat stunned for a minute instead of getting out to open Rose's door as he meant to. In this brief delay, Rose walked around the truck and let herself in and they drove off toward the country bar for what they both hoped would be a fun-filled evening celebrating the end of the old year and ushering in the renewed hopes and dreams of a new year.

The country bar had a great country-rock band playing and in-between sets there were people teaching others how to line-dance with music from the jukebox. The place was packed for New Year's Eve and the drink specials were amazing, Rose thought. She rarely relaxed enough to 'let her hair down,' but she did tonight. After two margaritas it was easier for her to have fun. She danced in the line dances with Ryan's friends and she even danced with Ryan a few times when he asked. She was starting to think of Ryan as not just her employee, but also a fried so she figured they could dance without being an 'item' so it was all just good fun. They danced and drank the night away. Ryan told jokes which kept her laughing. By the time the countdown to midnight, and a new year, came and everyone was given free champagne to toast with and Rose was giddy with merriment. As the bell tolled midnight and everyone was cheering and shouting, she lost herself to the rivalry... It had been a great night and a fun way to usher in the New Year.

Ryan dropped Rose home just before three in the morning. Even though she was a little tipsy, she was always careful never to drink herself beyond her reason. She got out of the truck and started walking to Ryan's side window. Ryan stepped out of his truck and faced her.

"Rose...uh..."

"Shhh." She put her finger to her lips in a way that excited Ryan as he hoped a kiss was to follow, but instead, she put out her hand. Ryan took it and she shook his hand saying, "Thank you for the great evening. You were right in making me go out. I do need to relax and unwind sometimes. I hope I didn't make a fool of myself. I must've had a little too much and got a little too excited with ringing in the new year. Good night." She let his hand go and turned and walked toward her front door.

She noticed that Lea must not yet be home as her car was not in the driveway. She wondered if she was staying over somewhere and regretted, she had forgotten to ask her sister about her plans. Even though her sister could be such a pain in the ass, she hoped her sister had as much fun as she had. She opened her front door and went inside without ever looking back at Ryan. If she had, she would've seen he just stood there watching after her. There was so much he wanted to say to her and he had hoped this might've been his chance. After all, she had kissed him passionately when the bells at the bar had rung in the new year.

Chapter Fourteen

"Men are like wine - some turn to vinegar, but the best improve with age." - Pope John XXIII

"Rose! Get up! Get up now!" yelled Isobel as she shook a sleeping Rose.

"Wha...? What's going on? I was fast asleep."

"Rose, the police called. They took Lea to the hospital. She's injured."

"Oh my gosh! What happened?" Rose said as she sprang out of bed and started trying to find her clothes.

"I have no idea. The police said they pulled her over for swerving while driving. They thought she might've been a drunk driver, but they said they found her trying to drive with multiple injuries and took her to the hospital for immediate treatment of her injuries. The officer told me she was not in critical condition, but she needed care. They didn't tell me what her injuries were, but they said it looked like she had been in an accident or a bad fight."

As Rose put on the clothes she wore last night and her cowboy boots back on, she could only think that it must be Colin's fault. She didn't trust him. She never had to give him a chance as his actions continually proved to her, he was no good. She tried not to, but she also secretly cursed her sister for being flaky enough to give a guy like Colin a chance in the first place. She knew her sister was not like her, but it angered her how Lea always went through life as if she hadn't a care in the world. She hoped her sister was okay. She didn't want to see her suffer, but she inwardly hoped whatever happened might be the wake-up call Lea needed.

"I'm going to start the car. I told Manuel to stay here for now." Isobel said and ran out of the room.

Before long, they reached the hospital. They got Lea's room number from reception and were told they could go see her. They took an elevator up to the third floor and approached the nurse's station. One of the nurses took them to Lea's room, but warned them she was under sedation and sleeping right now. Isobel took one look at Lea and started crying. "Ay, mi pobre hija." was all she could say as she clasped her hands to her mouth and sobbed. Rose stepped up and examined her sister closely. Lea had bandages on her face, she had two black eyes, a swollen and cut lip, her right hand was bandaged up with splints on two fingers, and it appeared she had large bandages across her chest. Rose was tough and was known to hold her emotions in, but tears started rolling down her cheeks as she asked the nurse what happened and what was wrong with her sister.

The nurse did not have too much information on what had happened other than the police officer who brought her in had said that Lea claimed some random drunk had beaten her up as she walked to her car. The police thought maybe she had been drinking and got beat up in a bar fight, but her blood alcohol level was well beneath the legal limit. The nurse told them that Lea had three cracked ribs, possibly bruised or punctured liver (they were awaiting results from tests and x-rays), two broken fingers, periorbital hematomas (black eyes) around both eyes, and multiple bruises and abrasions. The nurse told them her doctor had said Lea was in Fair condition and should heal well as she is young and in good shape. Although the nurse rattled off the injuries in a matter-of-fact way, both Isobel and Rose were breaking down on the inside. As tough as Rose was, she was deeply moved by seeing her younger sister lying inert and injured and she could not stop the tears from rolling down her cheeks. The nurse told them they could stay with Lea and made sure they had chairs and left them alone. Isobel and Rose sobbed and talked about Lea until they both fell asleep from exhaustion and grief.

 Although the curtains had been closed for darkness, the soft glow of the morning sun was peeking out at the edges of the window. With two black eyes, it was hard for Lea to open them and look around the room. She saw Isobel and Rose asleep in their chairs and a weary smile crossed her face. Later that morning as she awakened more fully, pushed the button to move her hospital bed into a sitting position, and tried to drink some water. These noises and motions roused both Isobel and Rose and they dutifully got up and went to Lea's bedside.

"Ay, Lea mi angel…" was all Isobel could say as her sobs renewed at seeing Lea and her injuries. Rose, who was better in control of her emotions now, gave a little cough and asked her sister if there was anything they could do for her. Lea tried to smile, but she was still feeling some pain. She managed to say she was fine and did not need anything right now. Rose noted that at least she did not have a fat lip or was missing any teeth. She gave a little cough again out of nervousness and then asked her sister what happened. Rose did not mention Colin, but she felt he must be behind all of this somehow.

"Rose…Isobel…it was just my own dumb luck. Colin and I had a great time going around to various places eating finger foods and listening to bands right up until midnight when we rang in the New Year together. Shortly after midnight, I decided I was tired and wanted to go home. I told Colin I was going and we said goodnight. He was going back to San Diego on his bike and I walked back to where I had left my car. I guess I wasn't being too careful and some homeless drunk tried to take my purse, but I wouldn't let him have it. I put up one heck of a fight, but you can see I lost." As Lea finished her story, she tried to smile at both of the ladies.

"Why didn't Colin see you to your car? That would've been the gentlemanly thing to do," asked Rose and Isobel nodded in affirmation of the question.

"I told him not to. Where we said goodnight, his bike was parked one block to our right and my car was a block to our left. We said goodnight and we each walked toward our vehicles. In hindsight, I guess I should've had him walk me to my car, but I figured there were so many people out partying for the New Year that I would be fine. Live and learn."

"Does Colin know what happened to you?" asked Rose.

"No. At least I haven't had a chance to tell him. I don't think the police know about him. If Colin knew, he would probably be here like you two."

Rose had no intention of calling Colin and instead went into her lawyer mode asking questions and analyzing her sister's answers in her mind. "Okay, so you got beaten up by this homeless drunk. What happened next?"

"Well, I guess I could've gone back into the bar for help, but it was two blocks back and I thought I was in okay enough condition to drive home so that's what I tried to do. I got into my car with some pain, but managed to get in and start driving home. I guess my eyes were swelling shut and I was feeling some pain...I guess I was swerving is why the police pulled me over. A nice officer named Deputy Knox realized I was beaten up and brought me here. I think they thought I was drunk at first, but I overheard the doctor say my alcohol level was really low, which is right because I only had one glass of champagne right at midnight."

This time Isobel asked, "Where is your car?"

"Oh! I have a slip of paper somewhere. Must be with my things. The police had it towed to a police impound lot, but I think I can get it any time since they are not charging me with anything."

Rose continued asking clarifying questions, but Isobel was practical and decided to find the slip with the information to retrieve Lea's car. She knew it would be expensive having it at an impound lot and knew they should get it out as soon as possible to avoid big fees. She walked over to the closet and found Lea's clothes and shoes. On the bottom shelf, she found Lea's purse and looked inside. She found the slip of yellow paper right on top, but just underneath was a bunch of loose bills of varying amounts. She wondered for a moment how Lea could get so beaten up and yet not lose any money, but she grabbed the paper and went back to show it to Rose, keeping her thoughts to herself.

The doctor said the test results proved Lea did have two cracked ribs, but her liver was not damaged and her black eyes and various abrasions should heal quickly. They kept her one more night as the results came in, but by the next morning, they discharged her. Rose and Manuel had gone together to get Lea's car out of the impound lot and Isobel brought her home from the hospital. They had Lea's room all ready for her to relax in and even made sure there was a basket of her favorite snacks on her nightstand so she would not have to get up and down so much. The doctor had said her ribs should heal within a few weeks, but she should avoid unnecessary activity and take ibuprofen for discomfort. Her doctor said she might look pretty bad right now, but luckily most of her injuries will heal quickly although she will have to come back to have her broken fingers looked at.

As Lea tried to sleep, Rose came in to see how she was doing.

"Oops. Sorry, Lea. Didn't know you were trying to sleep. I'll go." said Rose who then turned to leave, but a groggy Lea stopped her.

"It's okay Rose. I'm glad when you check on me. I know you think I'm a flake and probably deserve whatever happens to me..."

"No, Lea. No one deserves to get beaten up for no reason. You're my sister and I do love you. I know we are not the same and we have many differences of opinion and tastes, but I do care for you. I always will."

"Thanks, Rose. That's nice to hear." Lea said through a fog as she had taken her ibuprofen and was feeling drowsy. As she was slipping further into her drowsiness, she began mumbling. "I love you too sis. I know I get upset when you are right. I envy your ability to understand people...must come from your law school training..."

"Shhhh. Go to sleep Lea. We can talk later." Rose whispered to her sister who was drifting off to sleep. She thought Lea was just starting to ramble.

"You were right. Colin was no good, but I'm done giving him chances to hurt me..." was the last thing Lea said before she started breathing heavily and was fast asleep.

Rose stared at her sleeping sister with two swollen and blackened eyes, two broken fingers in splints, cracked ribs, various cuts and scrapes, and so on. Lea's words brought the truth into focus and she felt like screaming at Lea to wake up and tell her more, but she maintained control. She could be wrong after all, but it sounded like Colin was behind her sister's injuries after all. As Rose contemplated what to do next, she heard Lea's cell phone buzzing on the nightstand. They had turned the ringer off to let her rest without distractions, but the vibration still made a faint buzzing sound whenever someone tried to call. Rose had a feeling and went to look at Lea's phone. The caller ID said 'Colin Bannerman.' With mixed emotions and increasing anger, she picked up the phone and answered without saying a word.

"Hello, Lea? Come on Lea. Don't be mad at me Baby. I'm so sorry. I don't know what came over me. I am so angry with myself for breaking my promises to you and hurting you. Please say you'll forgive me. I'll do anything you say to make it up to you. I never should've drank. You're my girl and I never want to hurt you. Please say you'll forgive me. Lea?" Colin said all of this quickly as he was afraid Lea would hang up. Rose wanted to say so many things in reply, but instead, she quietly hung up and dropped Lea's phone to the ground. She looked at her sleeping sister with mixed emotions then picked up the phone and put it back on her nightstand.

In a daze, Rose went down the stairs and Isobel happened to see her descend and asked how Lea was. Without looking at Isobel, Rose said, "That little flake. She lied. I can't believe she's as beaten up as she is and has the nerve to lie to all of us." Just then Ryan Alexander came into the living room as he was looking for Manuel. He had been told about Lea and was trying to be as quiet as possible so as not to disturb Lea, who he knew was recuperating upstairs. He stopped and listened as Rose continued. "It was that asshole. Colin beat her up, possibly for the second time, and she's covering for him."

Isobel shook her head and said, "No, Rose. You must be mistaken. This is too serious for her to do that."

"Colin called and I answered her phone. As soon as I picked up, he started pleading for her to forgive him for hurting her." Ryan did not stick around to hear anymore and he quickly left, unnoticed by either of the ladies who were too focused on the enormity of this new revelation.

Chapter Fifteen

"As you get older, you shouldn't waste time drinking bad wine." - Julia Child

It wasn't until the next day after Rose answered Lea's phone when she realized Ryan was gone. She had asked Manuel what he was working on and he sheepishly told her Ryan had stormed off to find Colin in San Diego.

"What the Hell will that accomplish? Men! I swear they are all so stupid. They say we are the impulsive sex, but look at what he does. He runs off to fight battles that aren't even his."

Manuel reached out and calmingly grabbed her arm and said, "My dear one, haven't you ever noticed how Ryan always tries to help you? He wants to be a friend to you and your sister. He respected your parents and was a friend to them, and now that they are gone, he feels protective of you both."

"But he shouldn't. Lea and I haven't known him for long. He shouldn't act like this."

"Rose, let me speak frankly. He likes you. He likes you very much. He feels he loves you and wants to do anything to make things better for you."

Rose was momentarily stunned by this blatant talk. In the back of her mind, she always felt that maybe Ryan liked her, but she always dismissed his behavior as just kissing up to her as his boss.

"He can't...he can't like me. I mean..."

"Why can't he, Rose? You are a pretty young woman and he is a handsome young man. What is there that is so difficult to understand?"

"I don't want to discuss this anymore right now. I need time to think," said Rose as she walked off toward the house and her room. She would need time to think. She was used to scaring men away with her independence and intelligence and could not believe this...field hand...this vine worker...could seriously be interested in her. Yet, she did have to admit he was handsome. And he had nice muscles and...no, she thought. She forced herself to think only about what he was doing right now. Ryan had run off half-cocked to...to do what? She didn't even know what Ryan hoped to accomplish in finding Colin. As she lay in her bed thinking, she tried calling Ryan on his cell phone, but it kept going straight to voicemail. On the third try, she left a voice message, "Ryan. I have no idea what you hope to do, but I want you to call me as soon as you can." She kept it business-like, and professional. She was proud of herself for not letting emotions sway her, but in the back of her mind, the seeds were developing into a small bud of thought about Ryan Alexander.

Ryan knew he was acting impetuously. In his gallant, yet simplistic view of life, he thought he would find Colin and either kick his ass or somehow make him atone for what he did to Lea. He had driven to San

Diego and to the university. He parked and spent hours walking around the campus asking various people if they knew Colin Bannerman or where he might be.

One young woman told him she knew who he was, but not much else. She said her friend Roxy knew him and she was working in the student commons right now. Ryan remembered Lea talking about her friend Roxy. He figured this might be her so he rushed over to the commons and asked for a girl named Roxy. One person pointed her out and he went up and asked her if she was Lea's friend. She said yes and asked in alarm if something was wrong with her. He told her the little he knew and asked if she knew where Colin Bannerman might be.

Roxy had no scruples about giving Ryan his address. It was just then that Ryan realized he did not have his cell phone on him. He realized he must've left it back in his room at the vineyard. Roxy went ahead and wrote down Colin's address and some basic directions on a piece of paper and gave it to Ryan. She watched as Ryan's broad, muscular back disappeared into the distance as he strode across campus back towards his parked car and thought Lea was a fool for not trying to date him instead of that loser Colin.

Colin finally got through to Lea, but several hours had passed since the call Rose had answered. Lea had seen his many missed calls and had ignored them, but she finally answered, but only after she realized she was totally done with him and he could not affect her decisions anymore. She answered his call and talked before he could, "Look Colin, I'm done with you. We...are...done. You hurt me for the last time. I believed in you and you let me down for the last time. There is nothing more to say."

"Lea, my girl...my living doll..."

"Cut the sweet talk, Colin. You hurt me enough that I realized how stupid I've been. I don't want to see you ever again."

"Lea, please..." he said as if greatly pained and through tears.

"Please what, Colin? Please let me hit you again Lea. Please let me lie to you again Lea. Don't 'please' me. I owe you nothing Colin. You screwed up. I would have done anything to help you, but you blew it. Go ahead and get drunk. Go ahead and drink and drive. Go do whatever you want, but don't include me. I'm not here for you anymore."

"Lea...I am sorry. Did you tell anyone what happened?"

"Oh, you mean like the police?"

"Well...yeah."

"No Colin. I did not tell them about you. I probably should've, but I guess that was either my final favor to you, or else I'm just too vain to admit I was duped by an alcoholic scumbag like you."

"Lea, that hurts. You know you're my girl."

"No. You're wrong there. I'm not your girl. Fuck that. Fuck you. Oh, and by the way, Rose told me that Ryan is looking for you."

"Why would that asshole be looking for me?"

"I can only hope it is to kick your ass. Bye dickhead. Never call me again." She hung up and did not answer any further calls from Colin. As she lay in bed, she watched a documentary about the life of Julia Child, the famous TV chef. Julia was quoted as saying that 'As you get older, you shouldn't waste time drinking bad wine' and she thought the quote should've been 'As you get older, you shouldn't waste time drinking bad wine or being with bad men.'

The rest of the day passed without a word from Ryan or Colin. Rose was frustrated that she could not get Ryan to answer his phone, but Lea was feeling better every minute she did not hear from Colin. It was like her self-esteem and confidence were returning and she was surprised at herself how she could ever have fallen for a creep like Colin. She reasoned that if she did ever love Colin, he really stomped it out of her. She also realized that while she often told him she loved him, he never once said it back even though she kept hoping for it. Late in the afternoon, Lea received a short call from Roxy, who let her know that Ryan had found her and was going off looking for Colin. Roxy didn't have time to talk as she had to go to her evening job, but she thought Lea would want to know. She asked Lea what it was all about, but Lea told her to call back when she had at least an hour or so to talk.

    Rose and Lea both had a hard time falling asleep that night. Around three in the morning, Lea's phone rang, and half-asleep she managed to answer it. She said 'Hello' and the person on the other end stated they were a police officer and told her that her boyfriend, Colin Bannerman, had been injured and that they were looking for one Ryan Alexander in connection with his injuries. They asked her if she knew where Ryan Alexander was at the moment. She told the officer she had been sleeping and had no idea where Ryan might be. The deputy made her take down his phone number and case number and instructed her to call if Ryan turned up. She said she would and hung up and went to Rose's room.

    She woke up Rose and told her about the call. Rose immediately tried calling Ryan, but his phone continued going straight to voicemail. After a few attempts, she left a message telling him to call her immediately as it was important. The sisters stayed up the rest of the night talking over the situation. Lea finally admitted to Rose that Colin had beaten her up on Yom Kippur and again at New Year's. Rose told her she figured as much.

    "Rose, I'm so sorry I lied to you. I...I...I thought I was in love with Colin and I guess I put up with treatment from him that I normally would never put up with from anyone. He really had me believing I was special. He kept calling me '*his girl*' and I guess I bought into the idea of us as a couple. I feel so stupid. It's been hard to admit the truth to myself, or to you, that I was blinded by love into accepting his treatment of me. I am so sorry Rose. I should have been honest with you from the start." said Lea and then she buried her head, sobbing, into Rose's shoulder.

    Rose hugged her sister tightly and wanted to say so many things. She wanted to tell Lea that she had seen so many cases just like hers at the courts. Domestic abuse between boyfriends and girlfriends, or even spouses, was common. Instead, she decided it was time to keep her mouth shut and just support her sister. She had spent so many years chiding her sister about her perceived bad decision-making, that she felt she should just keep quiet this time. Besides, a little part of her was content to know that Lea was finally over Colin and realized the injury he had caused her, both physically and mentally. She held her sister tight and stroked her hair as Lea sobbed uncontrollably.

    After a while, Lea calmed down and they continued talking about the current situation. Rose could not believe that Ryan was wanted by the police for assaulting Colin. She thought he was smarter than to do something like beating him up to the point where the police were involved. She could see him punch Colin, but not beat him up to the point he was in the hospital. Lea begged to differ. After seeing Colin's violent outbursts, she figured any guy could snap and go out of control. A part of Rose knew what Lea was saying was possible, but another part of her refused to believe Ryan would act that way. He was so nice. He was always so courteous and conscientious toward everyone. Then she remembered both Isobel and Manuel implying he liked her and she wondered if Ryan was just playing games with her as Colin did to Lea. About this time, Lea's phone rang and she saw the caller ID showed it was from Colin. She asked Rose what to do and her sister told her to answer it and put it on the speaker phone. She did as Rose said.

"Hello, Colin?"

"Lea?" Colin's voice sounded cracked and a bit distant as if he were groggy.

"Colin, what happened? We got a call from the police."

"Yeah. I'm in the hospital. I'm pretty beat up. I need you, Lea. I need to see my girl. I'm hurt, Babe. Please come see me. I put you down as my wife so you will be allowed to visit me."

Lea looked at Rose, who was shaking her head and moving her arms to indicate 'no way.'

"Colin, I told you we are through. I'm in pain too so that makes both of us. Did Ryan really find you?"

A sudden change in Colin's voice made him sound aggressive and angry as he replied, "Yes! Your precious Ryan beat me up and he will pay for it. I told the cops all about him. He will go to jail for messing with me. Make sure you tell that sister of yours that her friend will rot in jail for coming after me."

Rose looked down at the floor and avoided Lea's plaintive looks.

"Colin, you can't be serious. I don't think Ryan would beat you up."

"It doesn't matter what you think. It only matters what the cops believe. I might be persuaded to change my story though."

"And why would you do that?"

"Come see me, Lea. Let's patch things up. We're both hurting. I want you back. I'll make sure all charges are dropped against Ryan if you come visit me. I'll tell them I was mistaken or something."

"Tell me the truth. Did Ryan beat you up?"

"Like I said, it doesn't matter. My story will get Ryan in lots of trouble if you don't come and see me."

Lea looked again at Rose who was still focused on the floor, but she saw her sister ever so slightly shaking her head back and forth as if saying 'no.' Lea poised herself and with her renewed confidence she told Colin, "No. I'm not coming to see you. I'm sure whatever happened to you, you deserve it. If Ryan is to blame, he will pay, but somehow, I doubt he did anything wrong."

"Go to Hell you little bitch!" screamed Colin over Lea's cell phone. Remembering a line she once heard, she calmly replied, "See you on the way down" and hung up.

Rose and Lea talked some more. Based on what Colin was saying, they were both fairly certain Ryan wasn't to blame, but it would be Colin's word against his. They hoped he had a good alibi and Rose was getting more and more anxious for Ryan to call her back. A deputy arrived around seven in the morning asking for Ryan. Rose met with the deputy and told him, in all honesty, that she had not heard from him. The deputy shared a little information on Colin's condition. He sounded about as injured as Lea had been, but he had a broken leg too. The deputy asked if he could see Ryan's room and he was shown it. No Ryan. The deputy left, but only after admonishing Rose to call him as soon as she heard anything from him and he left his card. The deputy drove off, but only went a short way down the road before turning back to where Rose was still standing in the driveway. He pulled up and rolled down his window and said, "Ms. Baudin, I just received a radio call saying Ryan Alexander was just picked up by the San Diego police."

After the deputy left, Rose rushed into the house and immediately told everyone about Ryan being arrested for assaulting Colin. Rose hated admitting it when she didn't have a plan, but she said out loud she had no idea what to do. Isobel and Manuel, both told her to go to Ryan. To go see if she could help in some way. Maybe even post bail if he needed it. Rose wasn't sure about it, but the couple reminded her how much of a help he had been and had possibly helped to save the harvest, if not the winery in the long run. She was becoming convinced maybe she should go. He was her worker after all. And maybe she was a little worried about him. As she decided to go to Ryan, she grabbed her car keys and turned to the front door, and found Lea standing in front of it.

"Rose, I'm going with you. Stop, don't say a word. This mess is probably my fault because I let things go too far with Colin and I want to help clean things up. I'm going. Period."

Lea was right in thinking Rose did not want her to go. Luckily for Lea, Rose was starting to panic a little with worry for Ryan and did not want to waste any time arguing with her sister. Rose shrugged her shoulders and let out a quick sigh of exasperation as she said, "Let's go then. Get in the car." On the way down to the police station in San Diego, Lea had an idea and told her sister.

"I never told the police Colin beat me up and I'm not sure I want to now, but I could hold it over Colin's head. He did say if I would visit him in the hospital he would drop the charges against Ryan. I can tell him he must or I'll press charges against him." Rose did not like the idea of her sister having to face Colin again, but Lea kept arguing her case, and eventually, she gave in. They decided to drive to the hospital instead. Rose was going to accompany her sister, but Lea told her no. Lea said she felt it was time to face him on her own and prove to herself she was over him and he could not crush her spirit. Rose didn't like not going with her, but she gave in and waited in the car. Lea went in and got a lot of looks from hospital staff because of her injured face, but she reassured them she was fine and was there to see someone. She remembered what Colin had said about listing her as his wife so she told the nurse she was looking for her 'husband' Colin Bannerman.

"I believe the doctor is checking on him right now. Can you please have a seat and I'll go see if the doctor is done yet." said the nurse as she watched Lea sit down and then walked away. A few minutes later a middle-aged-looking male doctor came out and asked if she was Colin's wife. She said 'Yes' and he told her to stay seated for a moment as he sat down and faced her.

"Mrs. Bannerman…"

"Please call me Lea."

"Okay, Lea. I'm Doctor Murray. I wanted to speak to you out here for a moment. Colin is pretty beat up, but he'll be fine. He was extremely intoxicated when he was admitted and it turned out he had a high volume of alcohol in his blood. None of his injuries are critical and should heal well. I see that you look like you've been injured too. Were you with Colin last night?"

"No, but I was the night before." She fell back on her previous lie as she continued, "I got beaten up by a drunk on New Year's."

"So, you were not with him at all last night?"

"No, why?"

"Well, your husband was admitted a little after midnight last night. He came into the emergency room and said he had been assaulted by someone. A police officer took his statement. We patched him up and he stuck to his story about being beaten up. His injuries could have been done by an assault, but some police officers are with Colin right now and charging him with a hit-and-run accident. I probably should not say anymore and let the deputies talk to you. Let me get them."

"No. Please just tell me this, was he actually injured in this hit-and-run accident, or was he assaulted after all?"

"I'm not sure…" He started to get up to find one of the officers, but saw the plaintive expression on Lea's swollen face and decided to tell her, "The deputies are getting the facts together. The driver who was hit had found your husband's license plate had fallen off at the scene of the accident and gave it to the police. The police also had a perfect description of your husband because he had taken off his helmet and yelled at the driver of the car he had hit in front of several witnesses. He just admitted to the police he had never been assaulted by anyone. I really should not say anymore. Should I ask if you can go see your husband now?"

"But what about the guy they arrested because he said he was assaulted?"

"I overheard the officers saying they were going to have him released without charges. I really need to get back now and check on your husband. I'll send an officer out to see you."

"I need to use the restroom. Can you give me a few minutes?"

"Sure. Just let the nurse know when you're back and we'll get to you."

"Thank you," said Lea as she started walking down the hallway toward the restrooms. She kept on walking past the restrooms and went out to Rose as quickly as she could.

"Let's go Rose, now," Lea said quickly with a short breath.

"What's the matter?"

"Just drive. Go to the police station, they're releasing Ryan right now. I'll tell you everything on the way."

Chapter Sixteen

"A bottle of wine contains more philosophy than all the books in the world." - Louis Pasteur

With Ryan safely back at the vineyard with all charges against him dropped, the story of what happened was told to all. Ryan admitted he wanted to beat up Colin, but realized no good would come of it. He did find Colin's apartment, but Colin was not there. He decided to stake it out and waited in his car, watching for Colin to arrive. By the time he had come to his senses, it was getting late and he gave up waiting for Colin and decided to sleep in his car. He figured he would drive back to the winery in the morning, but he was awakened by a police officer who noticed the steamed-up windows.

He chuckled saying that at first, the officer thought it was just kids making out, but when he found Ryan trying to sleep instead, he ran a routine check and found Ryan was wanted for questioning on a possible assault charge. They held Ryan for several hours until they said he was free to go and released him. He said he was shocked to see Rose and Lea waiting for him in the lobby. He told them how he never saw Colin and the sisters had to fill him in on the rest of the story. Rose chided him for being so impetuous and also for forgetting his cell phone. He agreed she was right, but he tried to defend his actions by saying how a man has no right to ever strike a woman and so on. The truth, of course, was that he was falling hard for Rose and wanted to protect her and her sister. Although he couldn't say it out loud, Isobel and Manuel gave each other a knowing look and they were both silent allies of Ryan's from then on.

Lea was glad she heard nothing more from Colin although one night Roxy told her it had made local TV news about Colin being arrested for hit and run and supplying the police with false information. She made sure to block Colin on her cellphone and just wanted to forget him. She was also glad the police never tried to figure out who she was or her connection to Colin. Lea promised herself she would never again be swayed by a rebel with blue eyes again.

She spent the rest of January and February relaxing and recuperating at her sister's orders. Rose often would say to her she was lucky she was injured in wintertime, but she would need to be ready to work hard with the tilling and planting which would start in March. Lea was glad Rose was showing concern for her, even if she was sarcastic about it. After her trouble with Colin, she did want to make better decisions and she was more interested in respecting her sister's wishes.

She realized Rose could've helped her a lot more, but she had been the one to lie and keep her sister out of her troubles. She resolved not to do this again and started spending evenings sipping wine on

211

their couches and having conversations about life. Sometimes Isobel would join them and they would talk and laugh late into the evenings. For the first time ever, she felt her and her sister were becoming friends rather than mere siblings.

Rose, too, felt the bonds between her and her sister were strengthening. She had always cared for her sister, but she always detached her emotions to save her from being so angry at what she perceived as flakiness from Lea. She was glad Lea was coming around and talking with her more. She felt they were turning a corner in their relationship now that Colin was out of the way. That was the only thing she privately thanked Colin for. He was so bad that her sister came back to her.

The winery was not out of the woods of severe debt yet and she knew she could only make it a success with everyone, including Lea, pitching in to help make it a real going concern. She kept it to herself, but her private savings were rapidly depleting like water going down a drain. They managed to get the last harvest bottled and shipped out bottles from her father's previous harvest, but they really needed a good harvest again this coming season, or drastic options might need to be considered.

As it was, she felt she could no longer afford to keep paying Ryan's salary, but Manuel had come forward and said he would gladly take a reduction in pay as Ryan was outworking him. Rose did not want to do this to Manuel, but he reassured her that keeping Ryan was necessary. Ryan would not only help him, as his back still gave him trouble, but he would also prove a huge benefit in the coming season. She hated to admit to herself that he was right, but keeping Ryan on would make a big difference so she resolved to do so.

As Ryan busied himself with various repairs around the house and the vineyard, Rose started noticing him more and more. Although she was upset at his running off to find Colin, she finally admitted to herself it was nice having a man around to help with things. She was pridefully independent and strong and could handle any repairs around the winery, as she had always done, but having an extra pair of strong and adept hands was proving helpful. And he was muscular and good-looking too. She felt those were added 'features' in having him stay on.

Besides, she found out on New Year's Eve that he was a good dancer. She had had a great time with Ryan and his friends. He was fun and they were fun too. She knew she rarely let her hair down, but it did feel good. With a capable man like Ryan, maybe she could learn to relax more often and enjoy life. After years in the high-stress world as an attorney and now being forced into being a vintner, she was becoming exceedingly glad for any little respite she could get.

Ryan had been careful to give the sisters some space after their ordeal. He was also a little afraid Rose might now think less of him because he went looking for Colin. He had kept her messages to him on his cellphone and sometimes listened to them when he was alone. He felt a little ashamed to admit he loved hearing her voice, even if she was pissed at him.

As winter was giving way to spring, Manuel would often sit on the back patio sipping Baudin wine and staring at the stars. Ryan often joined him, but he preferred to drink beer after a day of work. After a couple of bottles of beer on the back patio one evening, he admitted to Manuel all of his thoughts about Rose, including the recorded messages. Ryan was afraid Manuel would laugh at him, but he didn't. Instead, Manuel took a long sip of wine and stared up at the stars before he spoke.

"Ryan, you are a good man. I saw how you were with Alain and Claire Baudin. You were always respectful and helpful. I feel you are the same with their daughters. No man in love…truly in love…can be considered a fool if the woman is worth his attention."

Ryan chuckled and asked, "Is that another one of your old quotes?"

"No. It is from my heart to yours. Call it the philosophy of my heart. I was the same way about Isobel as you are for Rose. I could've stayed in Mexico and had an easy life running the family business, but I couldn't stand the idea of being away from her. She never forced me to follow her, but following her is all I ever wanted to do. Nothing else matters. Do you feel that way about Rose?"

"Yes..." Ryan answered feeling a little uncomfortable.

"Then that is all that matters. I have never regretted being with Isobel. Even though we were never able to have children of our own and we had to leave our old life behind. She is my sun and I follow the sun for warmth and for life just like the flowers do. I like to believe you came to work here to get closer to Rose."

"You really have a poetic soul, Manuel. You're a real romantic."

"You are too. You are too. You may not give voice as I do, but your actions are your poetry. Don't be ashamed of them. They do you credit."

They both sat in silence, enjoying a small bonfire, sipping beer, and staring at the evening stars before Ryan spoke again.

"Do you think I'll ever get anywhere with her?"

Manuel laughed a little before he replied, "Yes, my dear boy. Of course, you will. She was worried about you when she could not get you on your phone and even more when she was afraid you were being arrested. She rushed to help you. That says something. Yes, you are getting somewhere. You want an old saying? How about *Good things come to those who wait*? Ha! So old, but so true. You gotta melt that iceberg boy, but once you start, watch out for the

215

flood." Manuel took another sip and continued staring at the stars until he heard a window open and Isobel called for him to come inside as it was getting late.

"That's the boss. Gotta go Ryan, but I will tell you this; Alain and Claire would be thrilled to know you were interested in Rose. They once told me they wished she would find a guy like you. Make sure to put out the bonfire, huh?" Manuel left Ryan alone with his thoughts.

January had turned to February and February dissolved quickly into March. It was time to start tilling the vineyard. Ryan had worked in vineyards most of his life, but Manuel still felt the need to tell him why tilling was so important.

"Over the winter months, our vineyard goes into a deep sleep. It is only when the weather starts to warm up in March that our sleepy little vineyard starts to awaken and this is our moment to prepare it for another season. We will dig the soil and turn it over to aerate it and bury any weeds. The roots and plants are then encouraged to renew their growing. They reactivate themselves for another season. As they do this, we will keep working the soil many times and we will watch closely for parasites, or any pests, and protect our reawakened vines. If we do our job well, we will be ready to plant or graft in April."

"Tell me something I don't know, Old Man," Ryan said with a laugh. Manuel started laughing at his own seriousness too and clapped Ryan on the back as both men went out to work the vineyard. Ryan had known Manuel for many years and knew he was a serious hard worker. Manuel was well-respected by all who knew him for both his industriousness and his loyalty to the winery. Ryan had worked with Manuel a few times when Alain was still alive and knew that although he was a slim and short man, he could work the fields like a Hercules. It came as a surprise to Ryan to see Manuel getting easily tired as they worked. He thought maybe it was due to his back injury and implored Manuel to go and sit. Manuel refused several times until he finally agreed to sit for a little bit. He told Ryan it must be the heat and he just needed to catch his breath, but when he felt better and returned to the tilling he again was not able to last long. The two men got to a good stopping point and Manuel said that was enough for today and he said he was going to go and lay down. Ryan put away the tools and ran into Lea who was out for a short walk.

"How's it going Ryan?" She smiled at him. Her injuries were all healed now and she once again looked like her usual self.

"Uh, okay."

"That doesn't sound too committal. Is something wrong? Did my sister chew you out for something?"

"Ha, no. Nothing like that. I guess I'm just a little worried about Manuel. He was really tired and winded today. I've never seen him like that before."

"Well, he is getting older and back injuries can take a long time to heal. At least that is what I've always heard. I'm sure he's fine. Whenever the household gets sick, he never does and instead nurses all of us. That man has a fantastic constitution. I think it's his Latin blood." she said with a joking smile.

"Maybe. We'll see. What are you up to?"

"Oh, just stretching my legs and getting some sun. With winter and being laid up in bed, I feel lethargic. Time to get my rear in gear you know. Shake off the cobwebs and get my bikini body ready for summer."

"Okay, Tiger." They both chuckled and made some small talk among the vines until Lea finally asked, "When are you going to ask Rose out again?"

"Do you think she wants me to? She was pretty upset with me about running off to San Diego."

"Ah, come on. She was worried about you which means she likes you."

"Manuel told me something like that too."

"So, what are you waiting for? Nothing ventured, nothing gained."

"What is with all of you and all your corny old sayings? Manuel talks like that all the time too."

Lea smiled and said, "Well, he is sort of our father now. Like Father like daughter, I guess."

"Another old saying? Argh. I give up."

"Good. If you give up, then ask Rose out."

"Why do you care? Why should I?"

"I know I've been a brat for much of her life, but I do love her and I want to see her happy. She's a tough girl and I've never seen her worried about a man like she was worried about you. Sure, maybe it was nothing, but it might be something. You asked her out on New Year's and everything went kablooey thanks to me. Did you have a good time with her on New Year's Eve?"

"Yeah, it was great. We danced, had beers, laughed, and everything. She seemed to have a great time. I know I did."

"Did anything happen?"

"I told you; we had a great time."

"You know what I mean," Lea said expectantly.

Ryan remembered the kiss he received as the bells rang in the new year, but he also remembered how he longed for another kiss as they said goodnight and only received a handshake. He didn't believe it was ever acceptable to lie, but he wanted to deflect answering this question.

"What? Like, you mean did she kiss me goodnight?"

"Yessss." Lea said with a twinkle in her eyes and her dimples at full strength.

"No. She did not kiss me goodnight." He avoided lying to her, but he didn't feel proud of it.

219

A few more days of working passed and it was evident Manuel no longer had the stamina he once had. Ryan was beginning to feel he should say something to someone. He did not want Rose to know Manuel was not pulling his weight with the work. He worried it might jeopardize his salary or Rose would get too worried about him or…who knows what. He decided he might say something to Isobel, but she had beaten him to the punch one night at dinner. They were all enjoying a meal together, Rose, Lea, Isobel, Manuel, and himself, when Isobel said to Manuel she noticed he seemed to have lost his appetite and was much too tired lately. She told him he was going to see the doctor to see how his back was healing and get a physical. *She told him*. He never questioned her when she tried caring for him so he took a day off and went with her to his appointment.

    Ryan and Manuel had completed most of the tilling and overall prepping of the vineyard for the planting to come in April, but Rose and Lea chipped in and helped him finish the rest of it knowing Manuel would be gone for most of the day. When Isobel and her husband returned from seeing the doctor, Manuel went straight to their bedroom to lie down. Isobel went out to the others and told them they took x-rays of his back and it had healed fairly well, especially for his age. The doctor told her he may still be tired from some residual pain from the injury and healing, but he wanted to run a bunch of tests on Manuel to make sure. She told them it might be several days to a week before they would get the results back from all his tests and it was obvious, she was worried. They all tried to make her feel better, saying it was probably nothing and not to let the waiting get to her.

Only a few days passed when she received the call from the doctor. She put Manuel on the phone. She watched his face as he listened to the doctor and only answered in grunts before finally saying 'Thank you, doctor. I'll be in on Monday.' and hanging up. She was used to his stoicism, but they were so connected she could sense something was wrong. She kneeled down on both knees in front of Manuel, who was sitting on the edge of the bed and looked up at him with concern and love in her eyes.

"Tell me. What is it?" she said and her husband reached out both of his hands and caressed her cheeks. He stayed there, holding her face in his hands and staring into the eyes of his sun. The streams started rolling down from her eyes onto his hands as he quietly said, "My days of following the sun are coming to an end, my Love."

Chapter Seventeen

*"Wine rejoices the heart of man
and joy is the mother of all virtues."*
- Johann Wolfgang von Goethe

    Cancer and death were coming to claim Manuel. His doctor discovered a large mass in his lung that was malignant and steadily growing. As the days wore on, Manuel started having difficulty breathing as the mass was pressing against his esophagus, partially cutting off his air intake. Isobel did everything she could to make her husband comfortable. She drove him to the doctor's appointments to see what they could do for him. His doctor did not dance around with his words but instead told them the facts in a matter-of-fact way which reminded Isobel of the actor Jack Webb and his deadpan seriousness when he played Sergeant Joe Friday on the old Dragnet TV show. Manuel's doctor was frank in saying the mass was too large for surgery to be an option and it was too late for chemotherapy to have a chance. He told them they caught this too late, the mass was growing too fast, and their best hope was pain management…until the inevitable end.

    Manuel stopped working and spent almost all the time laying down on his bed while his wife cooked his favorite meals and tried to get him to eat to keep his strength up. Isobel had always been a fighter, but she knew this was one fight they would not be able to win so she fought to make her husband comfortable and as pain-free as possible. Rose and Lea often checked with her to see if there was anything they could do to help, but Isobel would thank them and say something like, 'No. He is my husband and I am the one who must care for him as he always has for me.' The sisters knew she meant no slight against them. This was just her way, but nevertheless, they pitched in with cleaning and whatever they could to help.

    The sisters made their traditional Passover Seder meal which consisted of a stew of shank bone and egg, green beans, parsley, and a few other dishes including everyone's favorite, pineapple kugel. Even though the sisters were reformed Jews, they refrained from eating leaven bread during Passover and tried to stay as kosher as possible. Manuel was able to join them at the dinner table to share in the meal, the reading of the Haggadah story, the breaking of the matzah, and, of course, the symbolic drinking of four cups of wine.

    They had also invited Ryan to join them and he asked a lot of questions as he had never been to a Passover Seder before and wanted to know what each thing symbolized. Everyone was happy to see Manuel in good spirits even though he was starting to appear somewhat emaciated. He smiled and laughed along with all of them, but as soon as the dinner was over he excused himself and Isobel helped him back to their room. He had a good time, but he was tired and needed to lie down. No one mentioned it, but they all noted how little energy he seemed to have anymore, which was unlike the tireless man they had been accustomed to, and it made them worry for him.

    Ryan knew the best thing he could do was to stay busy and get as much winery work done as possible. As April began, he spent most of his time making sure the trellis system and wires were ready as the first new shoots started to appear. He was glad they had made most of the trellis repairs right after the last harvest and he could concentrate on planting new vines instead. The sisters offered to help whenever they could, but he told them they could focus on shipping and the tasting room now that the weather was getting better and customer traffic was picking up. Rose told him he could temporarily hire some of his buddies if he felt he needed extra help. Manuel, being invalid, made extra work for all of them, but no one complained.

    The winery received a large order from a local restaurant that wanted to start carrying their wine. The order was for twenty crates: ten of Baudin chardonnay and ten of their Rosé. The owners told Rose the last winery they bought from had been bought out by a large corporation and they wanted to deal with independents instead. The owners had also been at the wine judging and told Rose they were very impressed with their wines, which had a perfect blend of sweet bouquet and full, yet subtle, flavor. They gladly sent over full payment for the 240 bottles in total and asked if there was any way they could get them sent over today since they were only a few miles away. She told them the wine would be delivered within the next hour or so, no problem.

    She went out to her truck and drove it out back to the barn where the crates of wine were stored. Ryan helped her load her truck. He said he wanted to talk to her about something, but she said, in a stern voice, she was in a hurry to get the wine delivered and it would have to wait. Rose hated it when Ryan tried to corner her to talk as it really annoyed her. She got back into her truck and drove it back to the front of the house to get to the road. As soon as she drove to the front, she caught a glimpse of her dashboard clock and stopped her truck, and idled in the driveway. She was angry with herself because she had forgotten it was her shift to open up and run the tasting room.

    Lea had continued going on short walks and happened to walk back toward the house, finding her sister idling in the driveway. Rose told her the problem and Lea told her she could make the delivery for her. Rose was apprehensive at first, but Lea had been trying to be more responsible in running the winery so she gave in and got out of the truck. Lea hopped in and drove off. She knew exactly where the restaurant was and had no trouble driving there and making the delivery within the promised time.

The restaurant had some of their busboys come out to help Lea unload and the truck was empty in no time. Lea handed them a receipt to sign for the wine, which they signed and handed back to her. She got back into the truck and put the receipt on the seat next to her. She was about to drive off, but decided the weather was so nice that she would roll down the windows first. Once the windows were down, and she turned on some country music on the radio, she hit the road heading home. She had only gone a little over a mile when the wind picked up and the receipt lifted off the seat and started swirling around the cab of the truck.

     Lea panicked as she was afraid the receipt might fly out the window so she held onto the steering wheel with her left hand and tried to grab it with her right. She had been doing so well with Rose lately, she didn't want to lose the receipt and be thought of as irresponsible. With a big lunge, she reached out and managed to catch the receipt just before it seemed it would fly out the window, but her movement made the car swerve and she came close to hitting a parked car on the side of the road. She only enjoyed less than a second of triumph before she heard a police siren and saw flashing lights in her rearview mirror. 'Oh, shit' she mouthed silently.

     She pulled over immediately and the police officer pulled his motorcycle behind the truck and parked. He walked toward the passenger side window with his right hand at the ready on his holstered pistol. 'Shit...shit...shit...Rose is gonna kill me' is all Lea could think as the deputy leaned into the open window and asked, "Do you know why I pulled you over Miss?"

"Yes. I swerved. I'm sorry. I couldn't help it. I was afraid I would lose this receipt," she waved it in her hand as tears started to well in her eyes. With her voice cracking she continued, "I'm trying so hard, I really am, and I keep screwing up. Rose is gonna kill me for getting a ticket and losing more money." As she started sobbing and tilted her head away from the officer, he politely said, "I need to see your license and registration, please."

"Of course, here." She took them out and gave them to the officer who looked them over.

"The registration says the truck belongs to a 'Rose Baudin,' but you're Lea Baudin. That right?" From behind running mascara and tears, she replied a meek, "Yes. That's my sister."

"Stay here. I'll be back in a moment."

Lea could see in the rearview mirror that he was checking on her information. Before long he came back and asked, "Why is the receipt so important you almost caused an accident, Miss Baudin?' Lea couldn't help herself any longer and went into a long tirade about how she makes bad choices and she was never good enough for her sister and how her boyfriend abused her and...

"Step out of the car, Miss."

227

The officer's calm, but stern command made her stop blabbering and she could only mumble a weak 'Yes' as she got out and walked over to the officer. She looked up at this tall man who was wearing silver reflective sunglasses and had a tough, blank expression and was afraid of what might happen to her next. She didn't want to go to jail. The officer told her to sit down on the curb and she did as he told her. She was surprised when he sat down next to her and started talking calmly to her.

"You haven't been drinking, have you?"
"No sir. I was out making a delivery from our winery, but I have not had any wine today."

"Which winery?"
"Chateau Baudin Winery, sir."

"Oh yeah. I should've guessed with your last name. You don't remember me, do you?"

Lea had been frightened of this deputy and had not really looked at him, but now that she did, she still was not sure if she had ever met him before and told him so.

"Well Lea, you did meet me once. I'm Deputy Knox. I picked you up on New Year's Eve…early New Year's morning actually. You were in a Volkswagen Bug then."

"That was you? Yes, the Bug is my car. The truck is my sister's."

"Uh-huh. You seem pretty wound up. On New Year's you said a drunk had beaten you up. I'm guessing it was really this boyfriend you mentioned. Want to tell me about it?"

With sudden alarm in her voice, Lea said, "I don't want to press any charges."

"Okay. Several months have gone by since January. This is just between us. You seem like you need to unload and I'm almost done with my shift anyway. Go ahead. Just between us."

Lea looked at Deputy Knox, but she couldn't read him. What was he thinking behind his sunglasses, she wondered.

"You'd make me feel more comfortable if you took your sunglasses off."

Deputy Knox chuckled and removed his sunglasses and said, "There. That better?"

Lea looked into his eyes and saw that they were not blue, but a light brown.

"Yes. Much better with brown eyes…I mean much better we can talk eye to eye." She told the officer all about her parents dying suddenly and the responsibilities her and her sister now faced. She told him all about Colin and the truth about New Year's and why she just wanted to put it all behind her. She also told him about their financial worries and how Manuel, who was like a second father to her, was now being consumed by cancer. She somehow found it easy to talk to Deputy Knox, even to the point she felt glad he was the one who had pulled her over even if she did end up getting a ticket. When she was finished, she felt much better and thanked the officer for listening to her ramble.

"You're welcome."

"I guess you need to give me my ticket so I can get home before Rose worries about me being gone too long."

The deputy tried to look at her with a serious face devoid of emotion, but he could tell she was too happy now to be scared so he smiled instead and said, "No ticket. Be careful driving in the future. Here. Take my card and call me if you need to talk. I'm a good listener. Go on now and get that truck back to your sister."

On impulse, Lea leaned over and hugged the deputy and said, "Thank you!" and got in the truck and drove off. Deputy Knox stood up and put his sunglasses back on, got back on his bike, and rode off.

Lea never told Rose what happened and circumvented any questions by saying it took a while to unload because the restaurant workers were trying to decide where to store all the cases. It was a little lie, and she was trying to be transparent and honest with her sister, but the lie was necessary to stay on Rose's good side. Lea was so glad the officer had let her talk and didn't give her a ticket that she decided she would take him a gift basket of Baudin wines.

When Rose had work to do in the vineyard with Ryan, she grabbed a wicker basket she had and put in a variety of Baudin wines, and added some packs of crackers and various kinds of cheese they had in stock in the tasting room. She made a mental note to herself to make sure and list everything for their record keeping, but she stopped herself. She knew she would forget and this is why Rose thought of her as irresponsible. She made up her mind to go ahead and make a list of the items to be given away as 'promos' and left the list with the inventory paperwork.

She was proud of herself for acting in a way which Rose would approve of, but also because she understood the winery was her concern too and inventory meant money and must be dealt with responsibly. Responsibly? She almost laughed out loud at finding she was being responsible. She had to admit to herself it felt good. She put some cellophane and lavender-colored ribbon around the basket and drove off toward the police station.

When Lea had gotten back home after the delivery, Rose had gone out back to check on the planting. She stood on the raised back patio for a few minutes taking in the sight of the family vineyard on such a bright and beautiful day and she felt herself thinking of her parents and their struggle to make the winery a reality. She loved her parents deeply and was proud to keep the winery going even if she had sacrificed her law career. Seeing the vines awakening with new shoots felt like a new hope, a fresh start. Her only fear was how precarious their situation was. She had used most of her personal savings to keep the winery going after her parent's death, and although they were starting to break even, one unfortunate event could tip them over the edge. She thought about Manuel and realized she was losing not just his expertise, but also his labor. He had been with the winery for so many decades, working night and day, his loss would be tough to bear both in the vineyard as well as in her heart.

  She saw Ryan walk out of the barn and walk among the vines. She realized she had been a bit short with him about looking for Colin. She thought about just how much Ryan had saved them during harvest and how great he has been since. Although she trusted Manuel's opinion, she did not have high trust in most men and for months was waiting for Ryan to show her he was somehow not worthy to work here. Maybe he was an alcoholic, a womanizer, a drug user, a thief, or all of those things, but as she saw him in the vineyard, working hard for the winery, she realized he really was a good man. Right then and there she was resolved to be nicer to him. Besides, with Manuel unable to work anymore, she would make an offer to Ryan to stay on as head foreman. He had great skill in finding and managing pickers and Manuel said he knows all about making wine from growing to bottling. Ryan saw Rose watching him and he waved at her with a big dopey smile and continued working.

  With a silent sigh to herself, she decided to be nicer starting immediately and she went out to where he was. They made their 'hellos' and talked a little about how the vines were doing. She asked about some of the wines fermenting and he told her everything was going well and they were about to bottle the last of her father's wine from previous harvests.

Rose had not thought of this before and said, "This new harvest really signifies a new chapter for us then. From here on out everything is from our own doing, our own blood, sweat, and tears, as they say. Ryan, you know Manuel might not be with us for long and he can't work anymore. I want you to stay on as head foreman. Of course, there will be a raise and we'll have to discuss the whole package, benefits, and so on, but I want you to consider it."

He had been busy looking at what he was doing while she talked and continued to do so as he quietly replied, "Sure Rose. I'll stay, but on one condition." Her mental alarms were ringing as she quickly wondered what his demands might be, but she steeled herself and asked him what the condition was.

"I want to take you out for dinner and dancing next weekend," he said as he continued working.

"That's all?" she said with disbelief.

"Yep."

She was quiet for a full minute as he continued working the vines before she finally replied.

"I guess. Fine. Whatever."

He finally looked at her and smiled and said, "That's

great Rose. I know you always keep your word so I look forward to us going out. Where we're going will be formal so you'll need to wear a dress."

She had figured they would just go to the country bar again and did not figure Ryan would want to go anywhere formal. She was about to walk away when she remembered to ask him what he wanted to ask her about earlier. Ryan chuckled and said, "That was it. I wanted to ask you out." She wandered back into the house wondering if being nicer to him would be such a good idea after all.

Manuel was rapidly deteriorating as Isobel did her best for him. His breathing kept getting worse and the doctor finally put him on an oxygen tank to help him breathe. Isobel prayed and prayed, but she knew it was too late for any miracle at this stage. She knew she was losing her lover, her best friend, her steady rock and she wept every night, but only after everyone was asleep and she could sneak into the kitchen with a glass of wine.

Whenever Manuel was awake, she forced herself to smile and act as happy as she could. Manuel saw right through her, but wanted to see her happy even if it was a thin veneer masking her sadness. Her smiles and laughter had always brought him pleasure and he needed as much of both as he could get right now. He never realized how hard it would be for him to feel so weak and useless, but he was relieved Isobel was always by his side. It made dying almost bearable.

Chapter Eighteen

"When you are ready we can share the wine. Call me."
   - Deborah Harry (Blondie)

Lea happened to be on duty in the tasting room when she heard a motorcycle pulling up. For a quick second, she was afraid maybe this was Colin, but she realized this was silly and many guys around here rode bikes. Besides, she had not heard a word from him since she blocked him back in January and it was now April. She had just opened and this would be her first customer so she stood behind the bar with a big smile of welcome as the door opened. All she could see was the silhouette of a well-built man, definitely not Colin, as the bright sun from outside kept her from seeing any further detail.

"Hello. Welcome to Chateau Baudin Winery." The man stepped inside and as the door closed behind him, she saw what he looked like and realized it was Deputy Knox. He returned her smile and said, "I wanted to come and thank you personally for the nice gift basket. I got some ribbing from the guys at the station, but I think they were just jealous. It's not every day we get such nice gifts from people we pull over for swerving."

"Oh, it was my pleasure. It really was nice of you to take the time to listen to my problems and be so understanding. I really appreciated it, Deputy Knox."

"Bill. Call me Bill. Short for William. I'm not working today." he said with a big smile as he looked into her big blue eyes.

"You got it, Bill," she said, returning the smile as she looked into his warm brown eyes.

Later, Rose came into the tasting room to relieve her sister. There were a few customers languidly sipping their glasses of wine and chatting, but business was slow enough Lea had a few minutes to talk to her sister.

"Rose, do you remember me telling you that a Deputy Knox was the one who found me and sent me to the hospital on New Year's Day?"

"I didn't remember his name, but the rest…yeah. Why?"

"Well, he came in today and had a glass of wine. I thanked him for helping me and we got to talking and…"

"'And' what?"

"And he asked me out. Before you say anything, I know I shouldn't rush into seeing another guy after Colin, but Bill…that's his first name…is a deputy and not just some loser like Colin. Besides, I would be keeping my promise to you."

"What promise was that?"

"Not to fall for a guy with blue eyes again. Bill's are brown."

"Oh, Is that so?" Rose couldn't help smiling at

Lea's silliness. "Okay, do you feel ready to date again? It's really your choice. I just want you to date guys who will treat you right."

"I do think I'm ready. I'm all healed up, physically and mentally. I'm totally over that psychopath and I want to get back to a normal life. I don't think a date here or there would hurt. I'm promising myself to take it slowly this time. No more giving my heart to idiots who don't deserve it. I'm going to force myself to take some time to get to know a guy. I rushed with Colin and that was a huge mistake and I see that now."

"There's your answer then. You don't need my blessing, but I do appreciate hearing how you will try to be more careful with men. It's for your own safety. I worry about you, but I also want you to be happy. I don't think a date could hurt either. Go for it."

"Thank you, Rose!" said Lea as she jumped at her sister to catch her in a big hug. Rose was not the touchy-feely type, but she tried returning the surprise hug as well as she could. She was also happy thinking how much she saw Lea trying to be more responsible, with the winery and with men. She decided she might as well tell Lea about her upcoming date with Ryan.

"That's great news! He's been awesome around here and he's a real hunk too."

"Yeah, he's been a good help."

"Hey, have you ever told him that? I know you are not one for compliments, but you might want to tell him he's been helpful at least."

"I will. I know I'm terrible at handing out compliments and affirmations. I need to work on that. I'll tell him on our date. Oh, by the way, I offered him Manuel's position as head foreman. I probably should've included you in deciding this, but something came over me and I was afraid we might lose him at this crucial time."

Lea thought to herself 'Maybe you were afraid you might lose him,' but she did not voice this and instead said, "I totally approve. No problem. That is a perfect decision and I agree wholeheartedly with it. He's an awesome asset." She also thought to herself maybe Ryan would be the one to finally melt iceberg Rose.

-

By coincidence, both sisters were going on their respective dates on the same Saturday night. Ryan was going to take Rose to the fanciest steakhouse in the area, which was located at one of the local casinos. With her brunette hair, Rose dressed in a fancy red dress she used to wear to high-class lawyer dinners, which she felt complemented her looks. She was actually glad for the chance to dress up and she went all out with matching heels, black stockings, and even black evening gloves. As she applied her make-up, she realized it had not been since her date with Ryan on New Year's Eve since she had a reason to wear any.

She thought about what Lea said about him being such a help and knew she was one-hundred percent correct and she would make sure she told Ryan tonight just how much he has meant to them, his help and friendship. Although she had been upset with him for running off to find Colin, she secretly admired this as a chivalrous deed. It was just her practical side that worried about the legal issues if Ryan had found him and laid a finger on him. Her romantic side was buried deep, but it was there. She finished getting ready and went downstairs to meet Ryan, who was waiting in the living room.

As soon as he saw Rose descending the stairs, he stood up and was holding a single red rose. He watched her descend and involuntarily gulped as he saw how beautiful she was. He realized he had never seen her so dolled up before and she was really a vision to behold. Rose saw that Ryan was wearing a dark blue suit with a white dress shirt and red tie. He looked very professional, but she noticed he was wearing a polished pair of cowboy boots instead of dress shoes, but at least his pants legs were over them instead of being tucked inside them. He looked very handsome. What had Lea called him, a 'hunk'? Yes, she thought, he is a handsome man. It was then she realized just how good-looking, rugged, and muscular he was. He was built more like a football player than a farmer. She stepped down into the living room and said "Hello. Are you ready?"

"You bet. Here, Rose. A rose for a Rose." he said as he handed her the single red rose. She took it with a smile and said, "Let's go" and Ryan escorted her out to his truck.

The couple arrived at the steakhouse and Rose was alarmed to see the prices. Most steak dinners for two started at a hundred and twenty dollars and went up. These prices also did not include sides, drinks, or desserts. In her lawyer days, she would've been fine with eating at places this expensive, but she was not paying and she wondered if this dinner might be more than Ryan should really spend. She was about to say they could go somewhere else when, as if by mind reading, Ryan said, "I know this place is more than I normally spend, but this is a celebratory dinner, and when you celebrate you have to splurge a little. Please ignore the prices and order whatever you like. Seriously."

Rose decided it was best to be polite and give in as he was the one who invited her out, but she did ask, "What are we celebrating?"

"Why...you offering me the foreman position, of course."

"But we have not gone over the details yet. Your health package and benefits, vacation..."

"It doesn't matter. I know you are fair and honest, just like your parents. I see how you've treated your workers. I'm sure whatever you come up with to compensate me will be more than fair and I promise to earn every bit of it and never let you feel you got gypped."

"I made you the job offer. Can I at least split the bill with you?"

"Naw. I got it. Besides we are also celebrating that you finally consented to go on a date with me. Whatever this dinner costs will be worth it seeing you done up like you are. You're a knock-out, Rose."

Rose was not used to compliments from men. Men always thought she was pretty, but few ever remarked on it as she tended to intimidate them with her intelligence, independence, and stubborn aggressiveness when focused on something. She found herself a little surprised Ryan also seemed confident with her. After their wine was poured by the waiter and they were alone again, she decided it was a good time to compliment him.

"You look very handsome tonight. That suit looks great on you."

"Thanks. I guess I clean up well although I rarely get a chance to put on the fancy duds."

"You did well. You look like a million bucks."

"Aw, thanks for the compliment, but I feel like the Beauty and the Beast here. I mean, I know I'm beautiful so you must be the beast, right?"

Rose almost spit out her wine in shock, but she remembered Ryan often said things that didn't come out right. This must be one of his jokes.

"Pardon?"

"Just kidding! You're the beauty here and I'm the beast. Just had to rib you a bit. I know I shouldn't make jokes like that, but I guess I'm nervous and trying to break the ice a bit with some laughter."

Rose stared at him for a moment and then broke out in laughter which was infectious and made Ryan laugh too.

"You big jerk. I came close to pouring my wine glass over your head and walking out."

"Sure, but you're still here and laughing so I guess it worked."

They made a little more small talk before their meal arrived. They each had an order of French onion soup followed by the 40-ounce Porterhouse steak, with three sea salts, for two. All of this was consumed with a bottle of 2016 Chateau Montelena cabernet sauvignon which Ryan had chosen and was amazed at how well it paired with the steak.

"You did a great job in picking this cab. It's excellent with the steak."

"I know wine, Rose. I've been around vines and vintners all my life. I guess you could say wine flows through my veins instead of blood."

"Ryan, I'm not much for giving compliments, but I want you to know I truly appreciate everything you have done for us. We are truly blessed that you came into our lives and supported us at our weakest times. I know you knew my parents well and I'm sorry I never had a chance to meet you sooner, but I am so glad you are part of the Chateau Baudin Winery family now and I hope you stay for a long time to come."

"Of course. I'm not going anywhere. I'm all yours Rose." which he meant more literally than Rose realized at the moment.

Isobel braided Lea's hair for her date even though both she and Bill Knox promised to go on a casual date. He knew better than to take her to another winery so he asked if she would be fine with a nice dinner and maybe some club dancing afterward and she said that would be great. They went to a nice Mexican restaurant in Old Town Temecula that was converted from an old bank. It even still had the safe inside and the owners kept the wine inside of it with the door open as a display.

Lea felt Bill was easy to talk to as he was such a good listener. She loved how attentive he was to her needs and opened and closed doors for her and treated her like a princess. Lea realized she had to watch her mouth around him because she could swear like a sailor and Bill never used profanity. He told her he tries not to as it isn't a good habit for someone who has to speak to the public often. This got her thinking about his career choice and she asked him, "What made you decide to become a police officer?"

Bill looked down at his plate before looking back at her and replying, "It's going to sound corny, but I really wanted to do something where I felt I was helping others. I wanted to be useful to others and I thought stopping crime and keeping people safe sounded like a good way to do it. I know you hear about the bad cops, and we do have some, but I honestly believe most officers joined the force to be of service to their community and help others."

"Wow. You make it sound like modern-day knights in armor or something."

Bill smiled and said, "Sort of, I guess. I don't consider my work romantic like some feel about knights in armor and all that. At the best of times, I feel like someone's guardian angel if I am there to help them at the right time, or at the worst of times, I feel like a janitor cleaning up a mess someone has made. That sounds pretty bad huh?"

"No. I get it. It must be a tough job."

"It can be." He nodded his head affirmatively.

"But do you enjoy what you do?"

"Most of the time. The day I met you was a good day."

She smiled and said, "Thanks, Bill."

After dinner, the pair decide just to walk up and down the main road in Old Town. There were a lot of people out taking advantage of the cool evening spring breezes. Restaurants and bars were all open even though many of the retail shops were closed. Lea couldn't help thinking of Colin as she passed some of the bars they had frequented together. Bill bought them ice creams and they sat watching people going by as they ate and talked. She was feeling hopeful about dating Bill. She promised both herself and Rose she would not move too fast and she wouldn't, but she did feel Bill might be the one to win her over if he really was as nice as he seemed.

Colin had never forgotten Lea. His anger and the warped sense of betrayal he felt from her leaving him was beyond measure. It was consuming him. She was his girl. If he couldn't have her, no one should. He had thought about killing her after his arrest and his subsequent jail time, but he realized even he did not possess the capacity to do that. No, he thought, he would just hurt her any way he could. He had spent a few weeks in jail on the charges of hit and run, driving under the influence, and supplying false information to a police officer, but he was out now awaiting his trial. He knew he was facing some serious jail time and this might be his only chance to get at Lea. He had it all planned out. He sometimes partied with some stoners from Fallbrook and knew their pattern. They would drink and smoke weed all night until they passed out. They also hated the police and would give him an alibi.

On the same Saturday night, the sisters were enjoying their dates, Colin went to hang out with the Fallbrook stoners. He brought them weed and a few bottles of Jack Daniels whiskey. He made sure to start them off as early as he could so they would pass out. He pretended to vape marijuana while they used a bong. When they drank Jack Daniels, he had ginger ale in a pocket flask. As soon as he saw everyone was starting to zonk out, he pretended to pass out in an unused corner of the kitchen. This would not seem unusual to any of them and he knew he could easily go through the kitchen door to quietly get outside to his bike. He waited as some of the guys went to their bedrooms and a few passed out in the living room. When it was quiet, he silently crept outside and walked his bike about half a block before starting it and driving toward Temecula, toward Lea's place.

    He was careful to take as many back roads as possible. It didn't take him long to get near the winery, as he turned off his engine about a block away and coasted closer using the service road which ran behind the winery. He parked his bike behind some large bougainvillea bushes about half a block from the barn where the wine was processed and stored. He knew that this late no one should be working in the barn so he jumped the back fence and went into the barn.

    He was glad to find it unlocked and he used a mini-LED light to look around. He knew how to start a good fire and decided he would start one in the barn. He found the sprinkler shut-off valve and locked it in the 'off' position. He found a can of gas Manuel used for some of the gardening tools and used that and some packing material and unused wine labels to start a fire in a barrel as he had done before. He had a good fire going in no time and he positioned it in a corner of the barn where beams met and cleaning towels were hung to dry. He watched as the fire quickly ignited the hung towels and the beams started to catch before he left. He retraced his way to his bike and was gone before anyone saw anything. Manuel was awakened when heard a motorcycle start up out back and thought it was odd, but went back to sleep.

Chapter Nineteen

"Wine makes daily living easier, less hurried, with fewer tensions and more tolerance."
- Benjamin Franklin

Rose and Ryan left the restaurant and walked a short way to his truck. He went to get the door for her, but before he opened it, he turned and told Rose he hoped this would not be their last date. Maybe it was the wine, she thought later, but something within her urged her to give Ryan some hope. She moved closer to him and saw the reflection of the moon's light in his expressive blue eyes and all she could think to do was lean in and give him a big kiss that lasted a full minute. As she kissed him, it was like something snapped within her and she remembered how much she enjoyed kissing him when the bells rang in the New Year. Something just felt good about being with this big, strong, helpful man. Sure, she thought, all men act like children at times, but maybe he just needs the right woman to help him out. What was she thinking? She wasn't ready for a guy in her life. What with her sister to look out for, the winery...but his strong embrace and powerful lips made her reconsider. Maybe he is just what I need? When they finally took a step back, he held the door open for her with a goofy-looking smile on his face. She looked up at this big child and patted his arm and said, "Don't worry. This won't be our last date."

 Ryan was feeling ecstatic and trying hard to be as cool as possible as he drove them back to the winery. They both stayed quiet and only made small talk about how beautiful the evening was. Rose thanked Ryan for the wonderful dinner and forced herself to pat his arm a little. She was not used to being demonstrative with men, but she knew she had to try as Ryan liked it. She thought about what their date and kissing meant all the way home. She wondered if it was a smart move to date someone who she employed. Ryan kept remembering what Manuel had said about how Rose's parents would be thrilled to see her going out with him. As they neared the winery, they saw some flames through the trees as they drove near. They both mentioned something looked to be on fire, but they didn't realize it was the barn until they pulled up in front of the house. Ryan parked and jumped out of the truck and ran down the side of the house toward the blazing barn.

 Rose wasn't sure if she should chase after him, but decided to get out her cell phone and call the fire department instead. She quickly gave the emergency dispatch operator all of the pertinent information and was about to run after Ryan when Lea and Bill pulled up from their date. Bill asked, "What's going on?"

 Rose told him, "We don't know. We just got here and saw the barn was on fire. Ryan just ran back there and I just called the fire department."

Bill nodded and ran off toward the barn while the sisters followed behind as quickly as they could. Bill told them to stay back as he neared the open barn doors and saw much of the interior was in flames. He could not see Ryan anywhere and shouted his name several times with no answer. He took off his jacket and was just about to run in when the emergency sprinkler system kicked on and Ryan came running out with his right sleeve covered in flames. Bill thought fast and wrapped his jacket around Ryan's arm to smother it. Isobel, awakened by all the commotion, had looked out and seen the flames, awakened Manuel and told him to stay put, and ran out to see what was going on as she joined the others outside the barn.

    The fire department arrived within a few minutes and managed to put out the rest of the barn fire and called for paramedics. The paramedics on the scene quickly assessed Ryan was lucky as he had only second-degree burns which should heal easily. Just before the ambulance took him to the hospital for treatment, the fire chief came over and asked him what happened. He said he had no idea what started the fire, but someone had broken the seal on the shut-off valve and locked the sprinkler system in the 'off' position. He said he ran in and went straight to turn it back on, hoping the system would still kick in.

    As the ambulance drove off, the fire chief turned toward Rose and told her that a large portion of the barn was burnt badly, but that young man, pointing at Ryan, had probably saved it from all going up in flames. He also knew Bill and told him he was glad for his quick thinking in wrapping Ryan's arm. The fire department spent a couple of hours making sure the fire was completely out, checking the structural integrity of the barn, and making a basic investigation. It was past midnight when the fire chief declared the barn could be entered safely and would not be condemned, but there was massive interior damage. He also took Bill aside and told him, off the record, that it looked like a fire was started in a barrel intentionally and he would recommend a full arson investigation. Bill thanked him and returned to join Lea and the others.

    Although it had been a clear night earlier, the wind had picked up and dark clouds were starting to roll in. Bill told everyone they might as well turn in for the evening. Lea said she was too keyed up to go to sleep and asked Bill to come inside with her and sit up with her for a while, to which he agreed. Rose decided to change into her regular clothes and drive to the hospital to check on Ryan. Isobel went straight up to her room to tell Manuel what had happened. Isobel told him everything she had heard and wondered aloud how this could've happened. Manuel mentioned he heard a motorcycle out back on the service road behind the barn, which had woken him up, but Isobel had slept through the sound. He told her it sounded like the motorcycle engine started up and then drove off, which he thought was unusual. Isobel thought the others should know this as Colin came to mind. She went down to find Lea and tell her.

She found Lea and Bill in the living room drinking some coffee and talking. She told them what Manuel had said about the motorcycle. Bill turned to Lea and asked, "Does that mean anything to you?"

Lea thought it over and could only say, "Colin drove a motorcycle."

"Do you think Colin would do something like starting a fire?"

"Maybe, but I think he's in jail. He was good at starting bonfires."

Isobel cut into the conversation and said, "Remember how he pissed off Rose with his bonfire. I wasn't sure who was angrier, Rose or Manuel, over how Colin destroyed a brand-new oak barrel." Bill picked up on this immediately and asked what happened to the barrel.

Lea told him how Colin had made a bonfire in the barn for her and Roxy the first night she had met him. He used a brand-new oak barrel that cost a lot of money and basically made it useless for holding wine after starting a fire inside of it. Bill listened and was torn over whether or not he should tell Lea what the fire chief had told him. He took a chance, thinking Lea might know more which might help an investigation into the cause of the fire, and told her.

"Lea, the fire chief told me there is a possibility the fire may have started with a fire within a barrel."

Rose drove quickly to the hospital and was told at the emergency reception Ryan was now being seen and she would have to wait. Luckily, the wait was less than an hour before Ryan wandered out into the waiting room with his arm raised and lightly wrapped in gauze. He told her he did not have any open blisters, but he needed to keep his arm raised and was supposed to remove the gauze when he got home. For the first time, Rose felt she wanted to hug this man. He had received a personal injury from trying to save her family's barn and that meant a lot to her. She reached out her hand and lightly touched his face. She told him how the fire chief said he had probably saved the barn from total ruin and she thanked him wholeheartedly. He just smiled at her and said, "I guess this guarantees another date then?"

"I thought I already made that clear, but in case you forgot..." Rose leaned in and gave him another kiss. This one was not as long, but she made sure he knew what it meant. Iceberg Rose was melting and melting fast for this man.

The couple made it back to the winery just before it started to rain. They found Bill, Lea, and Isobel waiting for them as Rose had texted Ryan was alright and she was bringing him home. It was just past two in the morning and they all needed to go to sleep. Isobel went to her room first. Bill said goodnight to Lea and left saying he had to work tomorrow, but he would check on them. Rose knew Ryan would not be able to sleep in his room in the barn tonight so she made up the longest couch with a sheet and a blanket and made him lie down. She moved a coffee table right up against the couch, put a pillow on it, and made him put his arm on it to keep it elevated. Lea and Rose went upstairs to their rooms, but just before Lea went into hers, Rose asked, "Why didn't you give Bill a kiss goodnight? That didn't seem like you."

"Rose, I made a promise to you and myself not to rush into things. It might sound silly, but I told myself not to kiss Bill on the first date. I want to get to know him and make sure he is really interested in me beyond just the physical stuff. I like him a lot, but I want to take it slow and make sure we are a good fit."

"Sounds good. Goodnight."

Lea said goodnight and both sisters went into their rooms. As Rose lay in bed listening to the heavy spring rain outside her window, she thought about what Lea said and was pleased her sister was maturing in her relationships with men. Thinking about Ryan and Lea helped her get to sleep instead of stressing over the damage done to the barn. She knew she would have to deal with it, but it could wait until tomorrow.

The next day the winery was alive with noise and movement. The rain had stopped and it looked like it would be a partly overcast day as investigators arrived while Isobel tended to both her husband and Ryan. Rose was in the barn all day assessing the damage to their equipment and inventory while the investigators worked around her. Lea had tasting room duty, but she called Roxy first to ask if she had any news about Colin. She had very little to tell Lea other than she had heard he was hanging out with a druggie crowd and she had not seen him herself in many months. Lea was hoping maybe they could have a good 'girl chat' like they usually did so she could tell Roxy all about Bill, but this was not to be. Roxy said she was leaving right now to buy beer and head out with friends to go surfing. When they hung up, Lea thought about how different their lives were now. Roxy was still the wild university party animal while she was becoming a winery co-owner seeking stability more than fast kicks. Oddly, she thought, she felt good about where her life was going. The winery was giving her a purpose in life she had not ever thought of before.

    Unfortunately, the heavy rain had washed away any discernible footprints or tire tracks. It was determined a fire had been started within one of their empty barrels and drag marks were found showing the barrel had been moved to a corner of the barn where towels were hung to dry and the beams were low which helped the fire to grow, but arson could not be proved with evidence so the fire was labeled as accidental. Bill had Colin's whereabouts checked and the Fallbrook stoners said he was with them all night, which they actually believed as Colin had successfully snuck back as planned. In the end, there was nothing to do except put in an insurance claim and try to rebuild. Rose determined the smoke had tainted the wine in barrels which meant they had just lost thousands of gallons of product. She felt like screaming and crying at the same time. It was a well-known fact among vintners that while wine with smoke taint had no health hazards in drinking, it ruined the taste of the wine. This big of a blow might cost them the winery. Even if she could repair the damage and replace equipment before the harvest, they were at a major loss of at least a year's worth of income. All she could do was file an insurance claim and pray.

  As she waited to hear from her insurance company, she kept an eye on Ryan's arm and made sure it was healing well and he was doing exactly what the doctor ordered. Meanwhile, Manuel's health continued deteriorating. The sisters visited him as much as they could and even Ryan went up to see him a few times. One morning, Isobel woke up and checked on Manuel. He wasn't breathing even though his oxygen tank was hooked up and he did not respond to her trying to wake him up. She realized he was cold to the touch and must've passed away in his sleep. She couldn't stop crying as she went and told the others and the coroner was called for. It was determined he had been dead for several hours from natural causes. Isobel thought it wasn't natural for such a good and caring man as Manuel to be taken as he was, but she was a realist and knew this was the way of life. She would mourn Manuel's passing for the rest of her life, but she also was glad he had been a part of his life and knew she must continue living as he would have wanted her to.

On the day of Manuel Ontiveros' funeral, Lea and Rose were shocked at how many mourners attended. They knew Manuel was well respected, but they had no idea he had so many friends. From humble grape pickers to well-to-do winery owners all came to pay their respects. The outpouring of mourners paying their respects for Manuel was truly amazing to behold.

Bill and Lea had continued dating and he came to support Lea in her time of grief. To both sisters, Manuel had been like a second father and even more so over the last year since the passing of their biological parents. Rose, especially, would miss him calling her 'Little One' and sharing some meaningful quote he knew from heart. It had been a rough year for the sisters; the loss of their parents, Lea undergoing physical abuse from Colin, the fire, and now Manuel's passing.

Lea inadvertently gripped Bill's arm as she could not help but cry from all the tragedy. Bill held her and tried to soothe her as best he could. Rose held back her tears as best as she could. She wanted to be tough for Isobel's sake, but the tears came anyway. She was glad Ryan stood at her side and she reached out and gripped his hand. Ryan liked and respected Manuel and even let some tears stream down his face as the eulogy was read. Isobel stayed very composed, showing the inner strength she had. Some tears escaped her eyes as well, but she would not break down. She had broken down enough and was glad Manuel was no longer in pain. It was their way, to be happy for those whose suffering was at an end.

 A few days after the funeral, the insurance company gave the amount they would cover. The barn had a low appraisal many years ago and the amount reflected this. Rose knew they could not rebuild, or even maintain, this amount and she would need to talk to Lea first and then tell the others they should sell the winery. She couldn't see another way out of their debt. She was too tired and frustrated to cry anymore.

 She was tough and she proved how resilient she was by starting to turn around the winery after her parent's death, but this unexpected fire was just too much. It was the final straw. The last nail in the coffin. She decided instead of talking to Lea first, she would include Isobel and Ryan in the discussion later. They deserved to know exactly where they stood so they could make their own exit plans as needed. She got all the numbers and facts together and would present her case to them after dinner, ironically, she thought, over some wine. She would plead her case to them like the lawyer she had put away. She wondered if her firm would take her back.

    Isobel did not have to cook that night as so many of her friends had stopped by with food for all of them, they had plenty to eat. They all ate together, even Ryan who was now a regular at the dining room table. They made some small talk, but they were all fairly quiet, lost in their own thoughts over the recent events. As soon as everyone seemed finished with eating, she suggested they share a rare bottle of cabernet sauvignon her father had put aside.

    The bottle had been saved by their father, but it was actually the last surviving bottle from their grandfather Alphonse's family's winery in France. The story was that after the Nazis were defeated and he could return to find what was left of the family vineyard, he remembered his father had buried some of the wine before he resorted to just breaking all of the remaining bottles saying how he would rather send the grape juice back to the soil rather than let a single drop moisten Nazi lips. He dug up a crate that was from the final harvest of 1941 and brought it with him to the United States and kept it for special occasions.

    Rose told them all she wanted to open this last surviving bottle in honor of her parents and Manuel, which she knew would keep anyone from protesting against opening it. She opened the bottle and poured some out for each person. Rose gave a toast to her parents and Manuel. They all took a sip and talked a little about the passing of their loved ones and how good the wine was. Finally, Rose felt it was time to plead her case to sell the winery. She started slowly, building up to what she planned just as she had with court cases. She needed them to see things the way she did and did not want to scare them into a reactionary position. She wanted to win them over and make them agree with her as if it were their own idea. When she finally had said everything she could, giving all the facts and statistics, she said, "And this is why I hope you all agree we have no other recourse except to sell the winery."

Chapter Twenty

"There comes a time in every woman's life when the only thing that helps is a glass of Champagne." - Bette Davis

    A lot of things clicked into place between the fire and Manuel's passing in April and the harvest that September. Isobel had shocked them all after Rose's statement about selling the winery. She told them how Alain and Claire were not always able to pay them during hard times, but they had always paid the premiums on extremely large insurance plans for both Isobel and Manuel. The original intent was that they, and their children, would be taken care of, always. The couple had been frugal and had large savings so Manuel's insurance money was not needed by her. He had a one-million-dollar plan and she offered to share this to save the winery. Rose and Lea balked at this, but Isobel told them this was where she and Manuel had planted themselves, and like a vine, she would not move. She told the girls that although she would never replace their mother, she would be the best second-mother she could be and thought of the sisters as the children she never had with Manuel, but had raised.
    After a lot of decision-making, Rose filed the legal work to have Isobel made into a co-owner. The barn was repaired and new equipment had been purchased to replace the damaged equipment from the fire. More workers had been hired and a security

fence was installed along the service road that ran behind the barn. They also made sure they put in the most advanced sprinkler system they could get. The tasting room was also enlarged and given some upgrades with the hope to draw more customers. They had been able to salvage some of the wine that did not have smoke taint and were surprised it sold quickly as word of their winery was increasing. They kept the Chateau Baudin name for the winery, but it was decided their chardonnay would be renamed Tres Mujeres, Three Women, to reflect the spirit of each of the women now running it. It didn't win the wine competition, but it came in a close second at 92 points this time, which secured their chances for increased wine sales.

      Lea split her time between going back to school for a Master of Business Administration degree and being engaged to Deputy William "Bill" Knox. Lea thought it was kind of funny how much she was starting to enjoy running a business and Bill was a great calming influence on her. He knew how to treat her well yet keep her grounded. It came as no shock to Rose when they announced their engagement, but promised to give it at least a full year before agreeing on a date to marry. They both said they had found each other and there was no hurry. Rose knew her sister well. Even though Lea was trying to play it cool, Rose wondered how long this engagement would last before she pushed Bill to the altar.

Isobel took care of the household chores and cooking as she had always done even though she was a full co-owner and the sisters offered to hire someone to do those things. She told them now that Manuel was gone, she was happy to look after 'her girls,' but she did start traveling with tour groups from time to time and always carried a small picture of Manuel in a locket around her neck so he would go everywhere she went. Sometimes she would take Lea or Rose with her if either were free for a week or two.

While Isobel and Lea were vacationing together on a one-week Caribbean cruise, Roxy had called Lea and asked her if she heard about Colin. Lea told her she had not heard anything about him other than his alibi, which Bill had told her. Roxy told her Colin was about to face his sentencing hearing and it was thought he would get at least three to five years of hard time because he had priors. Lea said she could care less as she had Bill in her life now.

Two nights before Colin's hearing he was hanging out with his friends in Fallbrook and died of an apparent fentanyl overdose from marijuana laced with the dangerous substance. Roxy called again and related this new development. While Lea wanted Colin to face justice, she felt bad for him. She knew he had a bad childhood and never felt much love growing up. Thinking about Colin, she decided to pity him and let any residual anger with him fall away. In a way, she was glad his suffering was over just like Isobel felt for

Manuel's passing. It was time to move on and she felt Bill was the one to move on with. She was happy to be Bill's girl now. She knew that one day soon, they would all be drinking champagne instead of wine.

As she sat on the back patio drinking a glass of Baudin family wine, Rose thought of her parents and realized it had been a challenging year overall and was glad things were finally coming together. For the first time in years, she felt truly happy and glad to be alive. More than she had ever felt as a lawyer. She wondered what Manuel would have said then laughed a little to herself as she knew he would've said something like, *'Just like with the grape vines. As one vine dies, another is planted which will grow, ripen, and bear fruit before its passing.'* Something about the circle of life.

Although she missed her parents and Manuel terribly, she knew it was the way of things. It was her turn to live and bear fruit. She looked over and saw Ryan working among the vines. He was cleaning up the post-harvest detritus. She smiled thinking about him.

They were regularly dating now, but kept their relationship on a professional level during working hours. Sure, there were occasional slip-ups where they would disappear for a while, but they were working on where their relationship might eventually go. Rose even started thinking she might have children of her own someday, which she had never thought of previously and laughed at the idea of her bearing her own fruit. Ryan fully healed from his burns and as muscular as a racehorse imbued with the stamina of a bull, worked as hard as ever to ensure the winery ran smoothly. As always, he noticed when Rose watched him work and he always gave her a quick wave, but now he always blew a kiss her way too.

Author Notes

This story is purely fictional, but like any good fiction, there is some truth. I live near the Temecula Valley, which is known for its historic old town and the many wineries dotting the landscape. The Temecula Valley has become the Napa of Southern California over the last twenty years and continues to grow as new wineries are developed. It is also a favorite spot of mine to hang out at any one of the many great wineries dotting the landscape.

The Baudin sisters have some resemblance to a certain pair of French-American Jewish sisters I have come to know quite intimately, but I will leave their privacy intact and say no more. The men, good and bad, are composites of some men I have known in my life and I will keep their privacy intact as well. Some of the dialogue, such as when Ryan is talking at his date-night dinner with Rose, is very close to actual words I have heard on dates. I find the truest humor is that which comes from people and is not just fiction.

As far as what fiction inspired me, I can't say for sure, but two possible sources were the film version of Under the Tuscan Sun, which has no similarities to my story, and the Australian television show McLeod's Daughters, which bears a little more similarity, but not much. I'm not sure how the former inspired me, but during my writing, I kept referring to it with others. I can only think it is the portrayal of an independent woman who is facing mounting challenges, but has the determination to surmount them all and carve out a happy existence in the end. As for the latter inspiration, it is also a great example of how a diverse group of women comes to rely on each other when faced with the death of a parent, of two of them, who leaves them a working farm in the Australian Outback.

And, of course, I am a lover of good wine.

Quotes

Each chapter has a quote that matches what is happening within each chapter. Here they are in order:

"Where there is no wine, there is no love."
- Euripides

"Give me wine to wash me clean of the weather-stains of cares."
- Ralph Waldo Emerson

"Wine is constant proof that God loves us and loves to see us happy."
- Benjamin Franklin

"Sorrow can be alleviated by good sleep, a bath, and a glass of wine."
-Thomas Aquinas

"I drank to drown my pain, but the damned pain learned how to swim…"
- Frida Kahlo

"He who loves not women, wine, and song remains a fool his whole life long."
- Martin Luther

"Enjoying fine food and wine at the family table, surrounded by your loved ones and friends, is not just a joy -It's one of the highest forms of living."
- Robert Mondavi

"Most days I juggle everything quite well, on the other days there's always red wine."
- Rachael Bermingham

"I cook with wine, sometimes I even add it to the food."
- W.C. Fields

"Wine is sunlight, held together by water."
- Galileo Galilei

"Winter gives me something to wine about."
- Anonymous

"In vino veritas - In wine there is truth."
- Pliny the Elder

"There must be always wine and fellowship or we are truly lost."
- Ann Fairbairn

"Men are like wine - some turn to vinegar, but the best improve with age."
- Pope John XXIII

"As you get older, you shouldn't waste time drinking bad wine."
- Julia Child

"A bottle of wine contains more philosophy than all the books in the world."
- Louis Pasteur

"Wine rejoices the heart of man and joy is the mother of all virtues."
- Johann Wolfgang von Goethe

"When you are ready, we can share the wine. Call me."
- Deborah Harry (Blondie)

"Wine makes daily living easier, less hurried, with fewer tensions and more tolerance."
- Benjamin Franklin

"There comes a time in every woman's life when the only thing that helps is a glass of Champagne."
- Bette Davis

I love wine quotes and there were a few others I kept on a list to use for the right chapter, but I never had the chance to use them. I am including them here just for fun:

"A bottle of white wine. White wine and you."
- Iggy Pop

"Wine…the intellectual part of the meal."
- Alexandre Dumas

"Wine, it's in my veins and I can't get it out."
- Burgess Meredith

"Wine represents to me sharing and good times and a celebration of life. It is always around happy occasions with family and friends and centered around joy. What better item to be involved in then something that represents all these wonderful things."
- Dan Akroyd

"A meal without wine is like a day without sunshine."
- Anthelme Brillat-Savarin

Manufactured by Amazon.ca
Bolton, ON